The Horror Begins...

"Can't you smell it?" He whispered.

She could: an acrid smell. And it was growing stronger. Her eyes searched the shadows.

She saw them first. Two abreast down the narrow trail they came, horribly elongated beings with bone-white skins and cylindrical bodies no bigger around than her thigh.

Soon a pile of corpses choked the path. When Griggs and Consuela ran out of ammunition, they used their weapons as bludgeons to carry on the carnage. Finally, so weary they could no longer lift their leaden arms, they let them fall to their sides.

Consuela closed her eyes and slumped against Griggs. He turned away his head as the grinning things engulfed them and they were drowned in a sea of soft little baby hands...

The Grotto of the Formigans

Daniel da Cruz

A Del Rey Book

BALLANTINE BOOKS • NEW YORK

To Nikula Jirjis Shaheen,
Scholar, Gentleman, Beloved Jiddo

1

"Why me?" Griggs had asked.

The hard, lean little South African with sun-seared skin removed the bulldog pipe from his mouth and plowed up the ashes with a kitchen match. He knocked out the ashes against his heel. He looked at Griggs. "You're black. I need a black man."

"There are thirty million of them in this country," Griggs pointed out.

"With doctorates in anthropology? Ph.D.s who've written their dissertations on a black tribe of central Africa?"

Griggs said nothing.

"Sort of narrows the field, doesn't it?" The little man grinned crookedly. "Of course, there are other reasons, too. You're fit—seven years ago you ran 440 meters at an AAU meet in 44.9 seconds, and you look like you might still be able to break 46 today. Then there's that twenty months you spent among the Chamba doing research; it proves you can get along with the natives and take the worst climate in Africa. You have, in short, just the academic, physical, and racial qualifications we're looking for."

"I see," Griggs said. "That's why you want me. But you haven't told me why I want to go. As you probably know, we call this institution the Black Athens of the South. Why would I give it up to swelter for three years in the jungles of Zaïre?"

"For one thing, the mosquitoes in Zaïre have a slightly shorter wingspan," the South African said wryly, slapping at one which, gear down, was about to land on the back of his hand. "But there's a better reason than that. There are only four anthropologists in your department, and—"

"*Two* anthropologists," Griggs corrected. "The college catalog was edited by our instructor in creative writing. It lists Brennan as teaching comparative religion, and Doyle for theopneustic archaeology, but they actually belong to the Biblical Resources Department."

"Adds up to the same thing, Dr. Griggs: you're going nowhere in this bayou Bible academy, because there's nowhere to go. However, with three years of postdoctoral field research under your belt and a solid study on the Magenda d'Zondo to put some meat on your publication record, you could expect offers from some really respectable anthropology departments. In fact, we can promise it."

Maynard Griggs leaned forward. "Are you willing to put that in writing?"

"Of course not," the South African snapped. "I'm in the diamond business. In the diamond business, a man's word is inviolable. But I'll tell you what I *will* put in writing: the terms I have offered you, including an honorarium which is more than you'd make here in ten years as assistant professor. Plus all your expenses, of course. Any other questions?"

Griggs' eyes were held momentarily by the interrogatory gaze of the South African, then pulled away, to come to rest on the comfortable familiarity of the scene outside his open office window. There, on the grassy common, a group of students was flaked out in the shade of the great live oak, its limbs draped in skeins of gray Spanish moss. Snatches of desultory conversation drifted in on the warm, humid breeze. He couldn't hear what they were saying—for all he could tell, they could be speaking Chamba. In fact, now that he thought about it, the scene could almost be straight out of Africa, for the oak and its gossamer moss appeared, from this distance, startlingly similar to the acacia of the African savanna, with quelea nests hanging from its branches like Highland sporrans. Substitute loin cloths for the blue jeans, and the students could pass for Chamba herdsmen, taking life as it came, out of the noonday sun.

Black Athens, or Black Africa?

Griggs turned to the man from Pretoria. "Did you happen to bring that contract with you?"

That had been two years and ten months ago. Griggs had been in Zaïre ever since, except for thirty-day annual leaves in the United States, during the great rains.

The months had passed painlessly, even pleasantly. He and his two mates, a black paleontologist from Pennsylvania State named Joe Dickerson and a black mineralogist, P. P. Gambino, from Columbia University, had picked a bare hilltop in the transitional area between rain forest and veld, and there occupied a big, airy one-room house, with lots of screened windows for ventilation, and a roof of thatched cogon which blunted the piercing rays of the sun. From the veranda, they could look down upon a spring-fed water hole a mile away in the shallow valley, which then unrolled in a broad brown carpet across undulating savanna for hundreds of miles to the south, into Angola and South Africa. About 300 yards down the other side of the hill the dense tropical rain forest abruptly began rising like a green wall out of the lush grassland. Spilling into the Kwango River valley, the forest extended north to Zaïre's capital Kinshasa and far beyond.

They had constructed the house themselves, except for the roof thatched by local labor, building it upon a wooden platform resting on six-foot iron pilings. Not only did this allow the free circulation of air below, but kept puff adders, spitting cobras, boomslangs, wart hogs and, above all, the hyenas that slunk around looking for a handout, at a distance. The researchers themselves had access to the house by means of a narrow counterbalanced gangplank sloping up to the veranda, which they could raise or lower with a tug on the rope.

Inside, the house was a bachelor turmoil of footlockers and unmade cots under mosquito netting at one end of the room, and aluminum equipment cases and a tall gas refrigerator and range with their extra butagas bottles at the other. Against the wall reared a small mountain of cartons of canned goods—most of it Carlsberg beer—nearly reaching the ceiling. The intervening floor space was occupied by a drafting table and stool, two four-drawer filing cases, folding canvas chairs, crowded bookshelves, and specimen boxes overflowing with glassine envelopes containing samples of soil, sand, quartz, pyrites, pyropes, and ilmenites. A heavy work table served as their laboratory, with chemist's balance and microscope under bell jars, and racks of reagents on the wall above it. A battery-operated all-wavelength receiver hung from a nail on the wall. And, thrown or kicked into corners, were odd shoes, dirty laundry, love letters, bottles of insect repellent, discarded beer cans, sleeping bags, a two-man tent spilling out of its case, copies of girlie magazines, flashlight batteries, unfilled government forms, partially cured animal skins, and enough odd rocks to start a Japanese garden. The only decorations were a few family pictures tacked on the wall above the drafting table, a centerfold nude pasted on the lid of a packing crate that served as a dart board—its torso well perforated approximately where nature intended—and their prize: a desiccated pseudopenis of the female spotted hyena, nailed to the door, which a local shaman assured them would exorcise evil spirits and bring good fortune.

Well, yes and no. Nubile Magenda d'Zondo maidens, induced by small gifts to share their company from time to time, did indeed manage to exorcise the evil spirits of male concupiscence. Besides the lovers' catarrh that sometimes ensued, during their thirty-four months in Africa they suffered nothing worse than scorpion or centipede bites, second-degree burns from spattering cooking oil, twisted ankles, and the usual dengue fever, dysentery, and malaria, all in all a record of robust health for Darkest Africa.

On the other hand, so far as Dickerson and Gambino were concerned, anyway, good fortune failed to smile.

The three had been brought to Zaïre, ostensibly by the Fletcher Allen Foundation for African Studies (FAFAS) of New York City, ostensibly to make an in-depth ethnological survey of the Magenda d'Zondo, a tribe occupying some two dozen villages on the fringe of the Kwango valley. Dr. Maynard Griggs was the chief of the research team, concerned with the strictly ethnological aspects of the study. Drs. Joseph Dickerson and P. P. Gambino were specialists in stratigraphy and paleontology, it was true, supposedly seeking to reconstruct the history of the Magenda d'Zondo and other tribes of the area from paleozoological evidence. FAFAS had strongly suggested to the Zaïrian authorities that, if their theory was correct, as they had every reason to suppose from the study of fragmentary records, the three-man team would very possibly extend the record of fossil man far beyond that of *Zinjanthropus boisai,* beyond that of the three million-year-old Afar man, back as far as five million years. It would put Zaïre on the map, archaeologically speaking. Hearing that and remembering what the Leakeys had done for Kenya, the authorities immediately permitted the three Americans to begin work.

The facts were somewhat different. FAFAS was a front organization created by a South African diamond syndicate whose name suggested the fermented beverage the three men and their native girl friends consumed in large quantities. Dr. Maynard Griggs, the titular head of the expedition, was actually window dressing, as was his study of the Magenda d'Zondo. The sole purpose of his researches was to give a plausible cover to Dickerson and Gambino while they sought the location of volcanic pipes, in which the presence of gem diamonds was indicated by interpretation of aerial magnetometer surveys in the possession of the diamond syndicate.

The optimism was not unreasonable: not far to the north of Magenda d'Zondo country is Tshikapa, the center of Congo Kinshasa's gem diamond-mining area while, 200 miles to the east, Bakwanga mines a substantial proportion of the world's bort, or industrial diamond. The syndicate's idea had been that, if Dickerson and Gambino turned up "blue ground"—kimberlite, which is to gem diamonds what cold mountain streams are to brook trout—it would then be in a position to open negotiations with the government for a concession before any competing diamond syndicate even knew they had been in Zaïre.

But the operation never came to that. For thirty-three months, Dickerson and Gambino crisscrossed an area of more than 1,600 square miles, mostly savanna, purportedly seeking archaeological artifacts to substantiate the hypothesis that ancient forebears of the Magenda d'Zondo had roamed this selfsame area. To provide verisimilitude for the occasional government inspector who happened by to cadge a cold beer, they attached meaningless Latin labels to the motley collection of bleached bones, flint chips, pottery shards and rusted spearheads they had picked up on their reconnaissances, and invited the visitor's admiration. The usual reaction was a blank stare, an incoherent mumble, and a suggestive look in the direction of the beer-stocked fridge.

Meanwhile, Dickerson and Gambino were compiling comprehensive maps and observations on the region's geology, whacking up tons of Congo rock with their sample hammers and examining it chemically and microscopically in the makeshift lab at home base. They then composed long, detailed reports which, after more than two and a half years of toil, all added up to the same sad conclusion: no matter what the magnetometer surveys said, there were no diamond pipes in the area.

Their work concluded, Dickerson and Gambino packed their personal gear, and invited Griggs to play one last bone-bruising two-on-one game of basketball, Geos vs. Anthros, at the hoop on the side of the house. That night they celebrated their departure with half a dozen giggling Magenda belles and a tub of beer, then rumbled blearily off into the dawn in one of the two Range Rovers.

Griggs was sorry to see them go. They'd been good friends and good company, if somewhat addicted to practical jokes—like gluing together the pages of his new copy of *Playboy* and nailing his boots to the ceiling and substituting crankcase oil for his pancake molasses and planting a small but irascible boa constrictor in the oven when it was his turn to cook. But Griggs had bided his time and paid them back in a lump on their last night in camp. When the party had got nicely raucous and chaotic, he had a couple of the girls slip out with his companions' wardrobes, and on the village sewing machine run triple seams up the middle of all their trouser legs, socks, sleeves, underwear, and other apparel. He'd have cheerfully served a week on a Georgia chain gang to see their faces when they tried to climb into their pajamas that night.

Still, it was good to be alone for a change. Without interruptions, there was a chance he could finish up his researches before the rains came, a full month ahead of schedule. He had contracted to provide a detailed ethnology of the Magenda d'Zondo within three years and, somewhat to his surprise, he was on the verge of completing the job. Writing it up would be easy, for his notes were precise and encyclopedic, covering the history, language, social organization, child-rearing practices, initiation ceremonies, physical variation, diseases, religion, legends and myths, music, kinship, taboos, rituals, arts, crafts, implements, political system, economy, food production, courtship, marriage, and personal status among the Magenda d'Zondo. Each aspect of the tribal culture filled from one to four notebooks which, written in Griggs' loose and jagged script, he kept in a locked teak footlocker in the corner of the room near his bunk.

The latest notebook to be finished, one on Magenda ritual which had taken five weeks to compile, he placed on the drafting table the following afternoon. He patted it fondly, as if it were a beloved pet. In a way it was, for the revelations it contained, and his penetrating

analysis of their meaning, was going to enshrine the
name Griggs alongside those of Sapir, Kroeber, Math-
iot, Boas, Garvin, Meade, Malinowski, Benedict and
Radcliffe-Brown. The Big Nine of anthropology was
about to become the Big Ten.

Admittedly, luck had played a part. Had he not
been a light sleeper, and followed his maid-of-the-week
when she slipped out of his bed that night and vanished in the jungle, he would never have witnessed the
bizarre Termite Reincarnation Ritual, as he had named
it, which was going to establish Griggs' reputation
worldwide. The Ritual had everything—mystery, savage splendor, cruelty, the dank odor of the primeval
forest, supernatural belief and human sacrifice. And
when he published his book, he wouldn't need FAFAS'
muscle to get him a job: he'd have to hire a Black Belt
karateka to protect him from all the academic suitors
who'd come calling with roses.

Savoring that happy day, Griggs kicked off his shoes
and plucked a cold beer from the refrigerator. He went
out to the veranda, dropped into the wicker chair, and
parked his stockinged feet on the railing. Down in the
valley he could discern dik-dik and gerenuk grazing in
the tall grass, edging toward the water hole to which
instinct would draw them before nightfall. To his right,
the spur of jungle that impaled the veld like a long jade
dagger shimmered as it simmered beneath the late afternoon sun. Overhead, vultures floated lazily among the
thermals of low-lying clouds which promised rain. But
they were lying: the rainy season was still some days
away.

Dr. Maynard Griggs, Chairman, Department of Anthropology, Harvard University. That had a nice ring
to it. Or how about Dr. Maynard Griggs, Dean, College of Letters and Science, University of California?
That would make up in esteem what it lacked in snob
appeal. He'd have to think that one over. No need to
rush into a commitment. He'd have plenty of time to
sort out the offers during his forthcoming lecture tour,
for instance . . . . He let his fantasies drift with the

clouds as he finished his beer. Then, with a sigh of contentment, he rose and padded into the house.

From around his neck he took a string with a key and went to the footlocker to deposit the notebook, which would be the last but one before his research was complete. He opened the padlock and lifted the lid.

Empty.

His eyes were uncomprehending, as though the image was perceived in some sort of visual foreign language. Numbly, he knelt and thrust his hand into the emptiness, running trembling fingers along the bottom of the footlocker, like a blind man groping for his cane. He looked at his fingers. They were covered with a white, powdery dust.

"Jesus!" he whispered, straightening. "*Termites.*" His fist smashed against the side of the box. The inch-thick panel crumpled, its paper thin surfaces all that was left after the termites had consumed the heart wood.

He flung the splintered box aside, and on his hands and knees blew away the white dust underneath. Then he saw it, a tiny hole, too small for a grain of rice to pass through, yet sufficiently capacious to swallow a lockerful of notes and three years of hard labor. He could have wept.

But first he had to be sure. He went outside, lowered the gangplank, and walked with sinking heart to the iron piling directly beneath the hole in the floor. Sure enough, a brown thin-walled tunnel, looking very much like a desiccated six-foot-long earthworm, snaked up the piling from the termite nest below the surface of the earth. He tore at the tunnel with his hands. It crumbled at a touch, and with it, his dreams of glory. . . .

By late afternoon, the mound in front of the house had grown shoulder high. Having begun with scraps of the collapsed footlocker, he had added empty food cartons, stacks of old magazines and newspapers, discarded clothing, broken furniture, and all the other odds and ends he wouldn't be taking along when he packed up to leave on the morrow since, with most of his notes destroyed, there was nothing to stay for.

He applied a match to a wadded newspaper and thrust it under the pile, then retreated to the veranda, pulling up the gangplank behind him. Brooding in his wicker chair, he decided to forgo dinner. Instead, he poured himself a double shot of whiskey. He regarded it somberly, then downed it in one gulp, making a wry face, for he wasn't really a drinking man. The welcome warmth of the whiskey spread through him as he contemplated the crackling flames and considered his alternatives.

They were pretty bleak. No notes, no book. No book, no celebrity. No celebrity, no job—including, most likely, his old job at the (huh!)—Black Athens of the South. Hell, after this, he'd be surprised if they'd have him in the Black Hole of Calcutta. And even if he had the stamina to repeat his three years in the jungles of Zaïre—which he very much doubted—FAFAS certainly wasn't going to sponsor him, now that their hopes of finding diamonds had been disappointed. If anything, judging by his luck, they'd sue him for breach of contract.

Directly in front of the veranda was a bolus of dung, deposited there by a passing elephant. To Griggs, it was symbolic of the way he felt at this moment, his future devoured by termites. Africa had a way of devouring everything—ambition, fortunes, dreams, individuals good and bad, species, whole races of men. It even devoured elephant dung, he reflected, as he watched dung beetles swarming in the bolus.

They were of the species *Heliocopris dilloni*, huge beetles weighing eighteen to the pound, with powerful legs and heads shaped like bulldozer blades. Nocturnal insects, they emerged with the setting sun, burrowing up through the soil and hauling down into their tunnels chunks of dung, on which they would feed. Right now, the bolus was seething with the glittering black beetles, hundreds of them fighting for their livelihood. Within half an hour the bolus, which now could fill a bushel basket, would be reduced to a layer of indigestible fiber, the size of a doormat. The rest would have simply disappeared, like his three years of research on the Magenda d'Zondo.

He muttered an appropriate curse, and got up to pour himself another drink.

It was then that he heard it.

It came from the south, the thin abrasive whine of a jet engine running rough. It sounded like a chopper, and a chopper in trouble. The aircraft was coming his way, doubtless attracted by the bonfire, a beacon of light against a carpet of darkness.

Griggs went to the railing and peered into the obscurity. He saw nothing. But as he continued to scan the dark sky, landing lights suddenly flashed on, two javelins of light aimed directly at him. The chopper was low and losing altitude fast. A moment later, as its lights were beginning to silhouette the tree tops of the strip of jungle a mile to the south, the engine faded into silence, and the lights vanished.

Griggs braced himself for the crash, and the fireball that would burst forth when the chopper's fuel tanks exploded.

He waited, not breathing.

Nothing.

Just silence, and the night.

2

Pausing only to slip into his shoes, Griggs bounded from the veranda onto the hood of his Range Rover, parked six feet away, as he did whenever too rushed to bother letting down the gangplank. The hood was dented with countless heelmarks, but these mattered less than the metallic clangor they produced, which invariably scared hell out of any snake which had taken refuge from the sun under the driver's seat. The noise always brought the snake rearing up, ready to strike. When that happened, Griggs would jump back to the veranda, grab his shotgun, and blast the reptile into shish kebab. Today no serpents showed, so Griggs stepped over the windshield into the driver's seat, and took off.

In a direct line to the point where the lights had disappeared, it was no more than a mile and a half, but in swinging around the narrow spur of jungle Griggs had to drive more than six miles over rough country. Ten minutes later his headlights picked up the glint of metal, and he veered off in that direction.

Not a hundred yards short of the solid line of tangled trees and underbush lay a dun-colored helicopter on its side, a total wreck, in a haze of unsettled dust. The rotor blades were bent like paper clips, the ground around was littered with a thousand fragments of the shattered cockpit bubble, and one door hung down drunkenly from a ruptured hinge. A crumpled, still figure occupied the pilot's seat. But there was movement among the shadows beyond, and a dirt-smudged, disheveled giant stepped into the glare of his headlights.

It was a woman, but hardly a member of the weaker sex. She was nearly as tall as Griggs, who was six feet two, and built like a sumo wrestler, with a good deal of the tonnage concentrated in breasts like the bisected halves of a medicine ball. Black hair in two thick shiny braids hung down to her waist, around which was a web belt and a holster containing a pistol whose butt was nearly as ample, so far as Griggs could judge, as her own. She wore black paratrooper boots, a field uniform of rumpled camouflage green with doodads on the shoulder straps, a smear of blood on her forehead, and a belligerent expression as she shielded her eyes from the headlights' glare.

"*¡Oiga!*" she rumbled in an authoritative baritone, "*¡Corte los faros!*"

Griggs switched off the headlights, and replied in the same language, "*Lo siento, señorita, pero yo creé que—*"

"*¿Es Vd. Cubano, hombre?*" she broke in.

Her tone puzzled Griggs. From her accent, she was definitely Cuban. Yet there was anxiety in her voice as she asked if he was, too. "*No,*" he said, "*soy norteamericano.*"

"*Ah, un yanqui,*" she said, arrogance replacing fear. "*Entonces Vd. es el hijo de puta qui nos ha derribada.*" Against the faint twilight, Griggs saw her reach for her hip.

The gesture, together with the words "son of a whore," left Griggs in no uncertainty about her intentions. Even as he heard the slap of leather, he flung himself sideways to the ground. The gun roared in the darkness six times in rapid succession, showering him with splintered windshield glass.

Her footsteps crunched toward him. He lay motionless on the ground, trying to look inconspicuous. Then she was standing over him, silhouetted against the dim light of the stars. Her outstretched arm pointed at his head. An instant before the gun went off, he kicked at her knee. She went down, hard.

Griggs scrambled to his feet, his head ringing like a Chinese gong from the shot that had whistled past his ear. He heard the click of an empty clip being ejected from the automatic, and the sharp snap of a full magazine being rammed home. She was on her knees, facing him. He took one long step forward and slugged her, leaning into it.

When she came around and sat up, shaking the dust out of her ears, Griggs was wearing the web belt and pistol, and trying to pry the body of the pilot from his seat by the Rover's lights, which had somehow escaped the fusillade. But the body was wedged tight.

"Don't bother about him," the woman said thickly. She struggled to get up, massaging a swelling jaw. "He's dead."

"Hey, you speak English," Griggs observed, dropping the limp, pulseless wrist. The man's forehead was bashed in, the blood already congealed. He was as cold as a Swiss banker's handshake.

"And damned well . . . serves him right," the woman wheezed, weaving toward him like a drunk. "If he'd landed . . . when I told him . . . after your shots smashed our rotor . . . instead of . . . I . . ." She staggered, clutching at her throat.

Griggs put out his arms to steady her.

She sidestepped swiftly and clawed at the pistol.

Griggs jammed his elbow into her eye, and stepped back. "Keep it up, sister, and I'm going to hurt you."

"So much as touch me once more," she declared, rising easily, "and you're up against the wall." She glared at him with her good eye. "Do you know who I am?"

"Sure. You're Cuba's Olympic shotput team."

She drew herself up sternly. "I am Consuela Millán y Gorgas. *Commandante* Consuela Millán y Gorgas."

"*Encantado*," Griggs said drily. "I'm Maynard Griggs, civilian."

"Or rather, *mercenary*—isn't that it, you miserable *gusano*?" A wistful smile stole between the swelling jaw and darkening eye. "Do you know what we do to capitalist dogs like you?"

Griggs regarded her with distaste.

"We starve them for three weeks, cut off their balls, roast them, and then feed them to 'em, with plenty of tabasco sauce."

Griggs shuddered. "Well, don't invite me—my ulcer can't take spicy foods. Anyway, if your playmates come looking for you here, they'll get the heat, not me."

"What do you mean?"

"I mean this isn't Angola, honey—it's Zaïre."

"You're lying."

"Suit yourself."

"But it can't be. We weren't that far off course."

"Check the tag," he suggested.

She walked over to the vehicle, and rubbed the

caked mud from the license plate. Then she threw back her head and laughed, a ripe Mother Earth laugh that made him forget, for a moment, that she was a *comandante* in the Cuban army.

But only for a moment. "Well, I'll be god-damned!" she exulted. "So you weren't the son-of-a-bitch who shot us down after all?"

"Nope. That was some other son-of-a-bitch." He brushed bits of broken glass off the driver's seat and climbed in. He pointed to the south. "Angola's about fifteen miles—thataway. You can hoof it, or you can stay and pray for the dead, or you can ride with me. I'm going in the other direction." He switched on the engine.

The woman hesitated, then started toward the helicopter. "There's something I must—"

"See you around," said Griggs, putting the Range Rover in gear.

His tone told her he meant it. "Wait!" she shouted after the vehicle, already moving away into the darkness.

He braked, and slowed down. A minute later she caught up and jumped in beside him.

"It'll only take a second, for Christ's sake," she entreated him. "If you'll only listen to me. I must go back. It's very impor—"

"Just sit still and shut up," Griggs advised, as he shot forward in high gear, looking for bumps to rattle her teeth on.

A pair of eyes from the dark, unbroken fringe of jungle had observed the noisy approach and crash of the helicopter.

The pair became a dozen a moment later, as the woman kicked open the door, stumbled out, and collapsed on the ground.

Twenty pairs of eyes witnessed, unblinking, the woman's attempt to shoot down Griggs.

A hundred eyes watched them drive off in the Range Rover.

When the Range Rover's lights had disappeared, two

hundred incredibly thin figures emerged from the
jungle and converged upon the wrecked helicopter.
From the multitude arose a muted murmur, like the
sigh of a breeze among the dry leaves of a woodland in
autumn. The murmur suddenly ceased as the full
moon, heretofore hidden by a solid bank of clouds,
broke briefly into the open. In a moment, the figures
vanished into the cover of the jungle, not to reappear
until the moon once again crept behind the clouds.

3

Ten minutes later Griggs pulled up at the camp,
climbed to the hood and vaulted to the veranda. Along
the way, he hadn't uttered a word, nor did he now.

When the woman entered the room a few minutes
later, Griggs was depositing her pistol and belt—which
besides the holster was festooned with first-aid kit, fluorescent dye marker pack, canteen, emergency water-
activated flashlight and combat knife—in a stout
aluminum trunk. He added his own small arsenal, con-
sisting of a Smith & Wesson .38-caliber revolver, a
Remington 12-gauge shotgun, and a Universal M1
autoloading carbine as well as all the knives and forks
on the premises. Securing the trunk with a heavy padlock, he displayed the key and dropped it in a side
pocket of his jeans. He patted it.

"Looks like you'll have to get into my pants, if you
want to get your gun out," he remarked with a crooked
smile.

"Don't hold your breath," she replied grimly. "Who
are you, anyway?"

"Already told you—Maynard Griggs. Boy anthropologist alone in the wilds of Africa among the savage Magenda d'Zondo."

"Magenda d'Zondo." She pronounced it as if it were the name of her beloved. "Then this really *is* Zaïre."

"Zaïriest country in the whole wide world." He looked at her sharply. "You don't seem exactly crushed."

"God, no! I'm *relieved*. Look, Griggs—I guess I owe you an apology. When I shot at you back there, I assumed you were one of those mercenaries who shot us down. After all, you said you are American, so naturally—"

"Sure. I'm American, and naturally you shoot Americans. Conditioned reflex."

"If you only knew the kind of things those people do when they ambush—"

"I know the kind of things *you* do."

She dismissed the accusation with an impatient gesture. "Oh, that was only talk. Whistling in the dark."

"Hey! You speak pretty fair English for a *cubana*. Where'd you pick it up?"

"New York City. I lived in the South Bronx six years before my parents decided they preferred warfare to welfare. Speaking of which, your Spanish isn't so bad, either."

"First language. Grew up in Spanish Harlem."

"Well, I'll be damned."

They looked at each other and smiled, like childhood friends discovering one another at a class reunion.

"Hungry?" Griggs opened the fridge and peered inside. Except for a dozen cans of beer, it was victually empty.

"I could eat a horse."

He handed her a can of beer. "Try this. An equine relationship has been suggested."

She downed it in two greedy draughts, glanced around, and tossed the empty expertly in a wastepaper basket halfway across the room. "Now, then, while you're looking for the horse for a refill, where can I—ah—wash my hands?"

"Anywhere," he said, "just as long as it's not against the wall."

She laughed, a throaty, not unpleasant sound.

"Right. Go outside, turn north at the first anthill and walk forty meters, preferably downwind. Then ask any pit viper. They know all the best pits. . . ."

When she came back, she found the card table set with two cans of tuna, two cans of baked beans, a box of soda crackers, a jar of kosher dill pickles, two cans of beer, a roll of paper towels, two spoons, and a large can of fruit cocktail for dessert. He stepped back to admire his table setting, and dusted off a camp chair with a headwaiterly flourish. "Dinner is served, Comrade. Yours is the clean spoon."

The woman fell to, eating fast like a soldier, without conversation, and only a speculative glance at Griggs from time to time to indicate that she wasn't entirely absorbed in her own thoughts. Whatever was bothering her, she didn't want to share it.

That was fine by Griggs. He had a more important concern: how to cope with the catastrophe of his lost notes. For a hopeful moment, he considered the possibility of reconstructing them from memory. But he abandoned that line of thinking when he recalled he couldn't so much as remember his mother's birthday, or even what he'd had for breakfast that morning. Somehow, he'd have to get used to the idea of having lost three years, but the reconciliation wasn't going to happen soon.

The woman finished first. She daintily dabbed at her lips with the knuckles of large, competent hands, pulled a pack of American cigarettes from her jacket pocket, and lit up. Between puffs she picked her teeth with a kitchen match and stared pensively at a dirty sock hanging from a nail on the wall. Finally she said: "I must get back to the chopper."

"To bury your friend?"

She shook her head impatiently. "The hyenas and

vultures will look after him. Nature's way. No, there are some papers I must get."

"Tomorrow."

She started to protest, but from the set of his lips realized it would be useless. Besides, she reasoned, in the darkness no one would ever find it, even if they were looking for it—as they probably were.

"Can we leave in the morning, early?"

"Sure, why not?"

She nibbled at her thumb. "Tell me, how far are we from Kinshasa?"

"Oh—about five days, the way I navigate the goat paths that pass for roads in this man's country. My partners used to make it in three. On the other hand, sometimes they almost didn't make it at all. Why do you ask?"

"I want to go there, of course."

"What for? Angola's in the opposite direction."

"So are three rebel regiments—not to mention their foreign mercenaries."

"The Americans." He smiled wryly.

"And others. No, all I have to do is reach Kinshasa. After that, I can make my own arrangements."

Griggs pushed his chair away from the table. "Well, lady, I guess this is your lucky day. I'm leaving tomorrow for Kinshasa. You can come along."

"What about all this?" She looked about her.

He shrugged. "Expendable."

She leaned across the table and touched him lightly on the arm. "You don't know how much this means to me."

"Forget it." She wasn't hard to take when she wasn't barking orders or trying to gun him down, Griggs decided. With her face washed, and a band-aid on her scalp cut, and the two top buttons of her tunic missing, he could almost forget that she was a *commandante*. She had sun-bronzed skin, luminous jet-black eyes, and thick black eyelashes. Her nose, curved like a Saracen's scimitar, and her stern, out-thrust jaw, gave the impression of a confident masculinity, but at this moment she seemed feminine enough. And when she folded her arms under her breasts, as she did now, leaning back in her chair, a lot more so. "Another beer?" he enquired.

"I'd love one."

As he got up to get a couple of cold ones from the fridge, she said: "Tell me—what brought you to this godforsaken place?"

He told her, some of it. He didn't tell her about the diamonds, though. That was none of anybody's business. Nor did he mention the destruction of his field notes by termites, which would have made him look like a hare-brained fool. He felt lousy enough about that already. "How about you, Conchita?"

"Consuela."

"Consuela. At a guess, I'd say you're a battalion commander."

"What makes you think that?"

"The way you handle a gun."

She laughed, an embarrassed little titter. "Actually, I'm a supply corps officer."

"Good deal. All the ex-supply corps officers I know own penthouses, Rolls-Royces, and change girl friends every ten days."

"Not if they are in the Cuban army."

"No money in it, huh?"

"Well, you might say that. On the other hand," she said, choosing her words carefully, "when I shed my uniform, I intend to have put away enough to last the rest of my life."

She didn't seem reluctant to talk. No, she wasn't a communist. No, she didn't particularly like army life—who did? America? Well, she guessed it was okay, but remember, she hadn't been there in twelve years, and from what she heard, it wasn't all that wonderful anymore. At least, there wasn't all that robbery and rape and welfare dodges in Cuba. No, she hadn't been in the army all her adult life. In fact, it was only when she had failed in the annual competitions in her fourth year in the conservatory in Havana she—.

"What instrument?"

"Why—piano," she said. "But only because it was a requirement. Actually, I was studying voice."

"Bass?"

"You really *are* a bastard. Contralto."

"Don't apologize," he said. "I myself can hit an F above high C."

"I'd like to hear that," she smiled smokily. "I wouldn't have taken you for that kind of boy, though. Shame I didn't bring my tape recorder from the helicopter."

Griggs got up and went to the filing cabinet near the drafting table. From it he produced an oboe. He stuck the reed in his mouth and let it soak in beer dregs for a minute or two. Then he inserted it into the instrument, flexed his fingers, and launched into the Andante from Haydn's C Major Oboe Concerto. His eyes closed, his face a study in intense concentration, he played with the hypnotic charm of a modern Pied Piper, who would entice strange and wonderful animals from their lairs.

And they came. . . .

And suddenly, in the middle of a bar, Griggs stopped. He looked stricken.

"What's the matter?" the woman said, rising in alarm. "Are you all right?"

Griggs wiped the sweat that had formed on his forehead. "Yeah, sure, I'm all right."

"Why did you stop?"

Griggs pursed his lips. He looked at her appraisingly. She wouldn't understand. She was a Cuban soldier. She lived in a world of harsh reality, not native juju. How could he explain to her? He shook his head.

"I want to know," she insisted. "What's wrong?"

"You wouldn't understand."

"Because I'm a soldier? Not all soldiers are stupid."

He laid the oboe down carefully on the table, as if it were made of glass. "Very well. What do you know about the Magenda?"

"What is there to know? They're poor, backward, cruel, full of superstition, just like all—I mean—"

"Niggers?" He laughed caustically. "But you're

right. Let me tell you about one of those superstitions.
It's about making music at night. Taboo. Daytime is
okay, but at night—absolutely not done, on the pain of
death. Funny, isn't it?"

"They'll *kill* you if you play music at night?"

"No, nothing like that. Listen. . . . One night, back
in 1924 or 1925, a safari of Britishers passed this way,
camping for the night near a Magenda village. They
had a lot to drink, and as usual with British males under such circumstances, they got around to exchanging
dirty limericks and singing old school songs. That's all
that is known, because the minute they started singing,
their Magenda guides disappeared, with the safari's
bearers right on their heels.

"Well, the next morning, the guides couldn't find a
single one of them. Didn't expect to. They'd warned
the Brits, *and* got laughed at, of course. And the Brits
vanished—all eight of them. It's all on official record."

"But that's preposterous," the woman burst out.
"How do you know it had anything to do with *singing*?"

"It did. I *know* it did. My ancestors came from this
part of the Congo, and four generations in America
haven't yet completely washed away my jungle instincts."

"You shouldn't have had that second beer."

He smiled ruefully. "I warned you that you wouldn't
believe me. But that wasn't the only incident, mind.
The most recent was five years ago. A Belgian lay missionary—guy named Jean Bercque—was living in a
Magenda village, fishing for converts. He had a cassette player and a stack of religious tapes, among
which his favorite was a High Mass he had recorded at
St. Peter's. He played it repeatedly to prospective converts, but out of deference to Magenda sensibilities,
only during daylight hours. One night, apparently while
suffering malarial delirium, he switched the player on,
and the voices of the Vatican choir suddenly boomed
through the forest. The village emptied instantly. When
the natives filtered back, at daybreak, Jean Bercque

had disappeared. His tape recorder was also missing. Superstition? Maybe, but why take chances?"

"What nonsense!" scoffed *Commandante* Consuela Millán y Gorgas. She strode to the open door, threw her shoulders back, and began to belt out an aria from *Madam Butterfly*. Her voice was true, resonant and, so far as Griggs could judge, very nearly of operatic quality. But mainly it was powerful, a 120-watt-each-channel voice.

Griggs was so shocked that, for a moment, he sat transfixed. Two seconds later he dropped her with a flying tackle. Their bodies rolled out onto the veranda in a grotesque embrace, the woman defiantly shrieking out her aria, Griggs clutching her with all his strength, trying to squeeze the breath out of her. When that effort did not quite suffice, he shut her mouth with his own.

That proved more effective. The sound of singing abruptly ceased.

Other sounds began . . .

From the edge of the forest 300 meters away, eyes peered out. Then the moon was swallowed up by cloud, and there came the scuttle of many feet.

4

It wasn't the moonlight that awakened Griggs—it had been shining brightly nearly the whole time. It was something else. His arms were empty. He smiled comfortably. About time—a little more of Consuela Millán y Gorgas and he'd be dead. He wondered vaguely what had become of her. Probably went inside for another beer, or for a stroll down the road to get rid of the last one. He sighed, rolled over, folded an arm under his head, oblivious of the splinters of the veranda's rough planks, and went back to sleep.

A rasping sound—sharp, rhythmic, metallic—awakened him the second time. He lay there while his mind lazily tried to analyze its source. Suddenly he knew. He got stealthily to his feet. Crossing the threshold into the house, the moon cast his shadow halfway to where she knelt, naked, by the aluminum chest in which he had locked the firearms and knives five or six hours earlier. But she was too busy to notice him until he was upon her.

"Why don't you try the key?"

She turned slowly, moonbeams reflecting off breasts which he had discovered, to his considerable surprise, did not yield even to gravity, but seemed to retain their precise and wonderful geometry in any position—and God knew he had tried them all. She struck him, absently, on the kneecap with the file. It hurt like blazes, but at the same time it indicated a conciliatory frame of mind, for if she'd put some muscle into it, he'd have been crippled for life.

"Griggs," she said, "I've just about come to the conclusion you are the world's champion liar."

"True. And you are the world's champion sucker, if you believe that the key I showed you was actually the one that fits that padlock you're pathetically trying to file in two."

"So, I'm the world's champion sucker, am I?" she smiled provocatively.

"You've proved it to my satisfaction, let's say," he elaborated. "What's with the file? If you wanted your gun, why didn't you ask? I'd have given it to you, you know."

She executed a graceful half turn to sit before him in the lotus position, about the only one she had not yet demonstrated. "Maybe I'd have shot you with it."

"Considering the shape you've left me in, sweetheart, that would be an act of simple Christian charity."

"Your shape looks all right to me," she drawled, inspecting it at first hand—whereupon the conversation languished. . . .

The fingers of dawn had begun to invert the bowl of night when they awoke at last, in each other's limp embrace. Slowly, voluptuously, they untangled their limbs, and Griggs levered himself to his feet, crossed to the stove, and put on water for coffee.

Breakfast, of canned peaches, soda crackers and Magenda cheese, and three cups of coffee apiece, found them washed, dressed, and ready to talk about something besides their mutually satisfying discoveries of the night before.

"Listen, Griggs, I've got to get to that chopper."

"Sure. It'll only take me a couple of hours to pack up the stuff I'm not leaving behind, and we'll pass by there on our way to Kinshasa."

"No, Griggs. Now. . . . Please?"

He regarded her suspiciously. "What's the hurry, Connie? It's not going anywhere."

"Those rebels know they hit us. If they're any kind of soldiers, they'll come looking for us. Every minute of daylight improves their chances of finding the helicopter before I can get my papers. I can't lose them. They mean everything to me."

It was the right sort of appeal to make to Griggs, who was thinking about his own loss of the day before. He shrugged. "Okay, let's go."

She kissed him once, hard, on the lips, and held out her hand.

"What's that for?"

"The key. You don't think I'm going to wander about the countryside unarmed, do you? If they captured me, I'd be raped by every soldier in northern Angola."

"All the worse for them—they wouldn't last till sundown." He took the key out of the bottom of the box of soda crackers and fitted it into the padlock. He opened the chest, handed her the web belt and holster, and took out the autoloading carbine which he carried when he expected to be away from camp for any length of time. He taped a full 30-round magazine to each side of the stock, and snapped a third into the magazine well.

Consuela meanwhile had buckled the belt around her waist. She pulled the pistol from the holster, worked the slide a couple of times, and jammed in a fresh clip, letting the slide carry a cartridge into the chamber. She shoved the pistol back in the holster, buttoned it down, and filled the canteen from the jerry can next to the fridge. "I'm ready," she announced.

"I have yet to see you when you aren't," Griggs replied, slapping her ungently on the behind. "Come on."

As they headed east, the savanna exuded the morning odors of dust, drying grass, animal droppings and decaying carrion which, by some unfathomable African chemistry, the vast spaces and rising sun converted into a fragrance redolent of solitude and timelessness such as the city dweller is fated never to experience. This would be the last time Griggs would smell it, before he started north through the jungle to Kinshasa. He drove slowly, to imprint the memory of it firmly on his consciousness. It was the best smell in Africa, a continent of memorable odors.

Not until almost six-thirty did they round the jade-dagger spur of jungle and double back toward the place where the chopper had come down. Griggs stayed close to the unbroken wall of trees, for he recalled that the helicopter had crashed less than a quarter of a mile from the forest edge. But as he bumped along, each moment expecting to see the remains of the helicopter, and not seeing it, he began to feel vaguely disturbed. He checked his watch. They had been driving for nearly twenty-five minutes since they left the camp. They should have reached the crash site five or ten minutes ago. Yet there was no sign of it. He glanced over at Consuela.

She licked her lips nervously. "Where the hell *is* it?" She searched the emptiness around them with restless eyes. "We must have passed it."

"I guess so," Griggs said, unbelieving.

"We *must* have passed it," she repeated. "Turn around."

She was right. It couldn't be this far along. He swung around, and started back the way they had come, driving at barely a walking pace.

Consuela stood up on the seat, bracing herself against the gaping windshield frame. She could see the line of trees on her left, interspersed with thick underbrush that made it virtually impenetrable. On her right, the veld stretched out to the horizon, as if reaching for infinity. The ground was rough but relatively featureless, with no declivity deep enough to conceal a heel-squatting native, let alone a helicopter. If it was there, she'd see it. But she saw nothing.

They drove on. Then, after a few minutes, a glint of brightness caught her eye. She tapped Griggs on the shoulder. "Over to the left."

He complied.

"Right here," she said.

He stopped, and she climbed down. She walked forward and then circled slowly in front of the Rover. Within the circle were strewn a thousand shards of broken glass. Griggs joined her, both silently searching the area around the fragments of glass.

"Look at this," she said.

Lying in the dust in a cluster that could have been covered by a sheet of newspaper were six brass shells, ejected by the automatic when she fired at Griggs the night before. Halfway between the shells and the broken glass lay the empty ammunition clip.

"That puts the chopper right there." Griggs pointed at a bare spot, devoid of the smallest sign of vegetation. It was also smoother than the ground around it. And a different color. Darker.

Griggs sniffed the air. Standing on the bare spot, he perceived a strong, acrid smell that he hadn't noticed before. It took him a moment to identify it, but there was no doubt at all that it was the odor of formic acid, the defensive fluid excreted by ants. "Smell it?"

She nodded. "Would you mind telling me what the hell is going on here?"

"I wish I knew."

"Helicopters don't just get up and walk away."

"This one did."

"Then where are its tracks?"

"Now, that's a good question." Griggs got down on his hands and knees and examined the soil. It was not compacted as hard as the soil on the periphery of the faint, darkish blotch. Moreover, the nearer he got to the edge of the blotch, the less pronounced the formic acid smell. None of this made any sense.

They climbed back in the Rover. Griggs drove on at a walking pace, in a precise search pattern, spiraling out from the faint blotch and using his own tire tracks as a guide to ensure that they didn't overlook a single square centimeter of ground. The spiral brought them, in time, to the very edge of the forest, but of the helicopter there was no sign whatever. Griggs was ready to give up, to mark it down as one of life's many unresolved mysteries, when an idea struck him.

He had been circling counterclockwise, which the driver of a left-hand drive vehicle does naturally while searching the ground as he turns, when navigating by his own tire marks. But, it suddenly occurred to him, what if the tracks of whoever, *what*ever, had made the helicopter vanish, had come from and returned to the forest? Circling to his left, he might easily have passed over these tracks *since the sun was at his back*; obviously shallow, and casting no shadow because of the low angle of the sun's rays, the tracks could well have been invisible.

He drove a few hundred meters westward along the margin of the jungle. Then he whipped the vehicle around in a U-turn and proceeded back the way he had come, in low gear. He explained his reasoning to Consuela.

"But why do you think they came from the forest?" she asked. "Why not from the other direction—out there?"

"Beats me, Connie," he confessed, "but look at it this way: if tracks led off into the veld, we'd have seen them, because we'd have come up to them when we were circling into the sun, and the edge of the track farthest from us would have cast a shadow into the track's depression. . . . Keep a sharp look-out now. We're getting close to the line from—" He suddenly braked to a stop and pointed.

From this angle, the spoor was easily discernible. Tiny tracks, seemingly by the thousands, streamed from the forest to converge upon the dark blotch where the helicopter had crashed. Each track was faint, almost imperceptible, where the depression of the paw—or whatever it was—cast the merest sliver of a shadow against the low morning sun. One or even a hundred of them wouldn't have been noticeable, but these tracks without number left no doubt in their minds. Furthermore, they were in a particularly significant array: along a front of a hundred meters they fanned from the jungle toward the blotch, as though channeled through a funnel.

He got down from the vehicle and inspected a single print. He'd never seen one like it before. It was oval, about five inches long, with five tiny ovals of descending size clustered at one end. It *could* have been human—if these humans had feet the size of a six-month-old baby's. He rather doubted that humans that small would be able to make a helicopter weighing several tons disappear into thin air, no matter how many of them there were.

Pygmies came to mind immediately. But Pygmy country was a couple of hundred kilometers to the northeast. Besides, they never congregated in such numbers. The food resources of the jungle, popular fancy to the contrary, are meager. The Pygmies can support no more than a widely dispersed clan in any single area; yet these footprints represented a multitude.

A thought was taking shape in his mind, and he didn't like it. And overpowering this thought was another: the desire to be far away, and the sooner the quicker.

"They must have disassembled it somehow, and carried it into the jungle," Consuela said.

"Who are *they*?"

She shrugged.

"Where did they get the tools?"

"How should I know, Griggs? It's your country, not mine."

He laughed grimly. "Not after today, baby. Let's get the hell out of here."

"No."

"Come *on*." He climbed back into the Rover.

The woman started walking toward the line of trees.

"Connie!" he shouted after her. "Don't be a sap. That jungle's impenetrable."

She paid no attention to him, but marched straight ahead.

He put the Rover in gear and caught up with her. "Listen, Connie, you can't walk into that jungle. It isn't Central Park, you know."

"Of course not. I wouldn't think of walking in Central Park. Much too dangerous."

"At least there the animals are in cages. Come back, Connie—don't be a sap."

She went on. They were less than a hundred meters from the trees now. Her eyes, like a sleepwalker's, were fixed on the jungle straight ahead. "Nobody's going to take my money," she said, half to herself. "*Nobody*."

"*What* money, for Christ's sake?" Griggs yelled, swinging the vehicle across her path.

"The payroll, you simple bastard," she shouted in his face. "The payroll of the 142nd Brigade—$311,-000. In cash."

"*What?*"

"I'm not in supply, Griggs," she said, her voice dropping to almost a whisper. She looked around apprehensively, as if fearful of being overheard. "I'm paymaster of the 2nd Division. At least, I *was*."

"And you stole the payroll."

"Yeah." She said it as if he had just divined the answer to a strange and baffling question. She seemed a bit surprised. "It was on the spur of the moment. We were flying up from Luanda to brigade H.Q. when the pilot—Rivera—said, jokingly, 'Jesus, Consuela, what a night on the town we could pitch with the scratch you've got in those two canvas bags.' And I said, half-jokingly, 'What town did you have in mind, Rivera?' And he said, flatlike, not joking at all, 'Kinshasa. And I've got just enough fuel to make it.'

"I said: 'Oh, sure, they'd never think of looking for us there.' And he said, 'They wouldn't look. That is, they wouldn't if they thought we'd been shot down by the rebs, when actually we came down just across the border, put a few bullets through the rotor and burned the chopper to make it look good.' So I said, 'Great, and what do we use for our burnt corpses?' Well, we kicked that around for a while, all the time pretending not to notice that we had left Brigade H.Q. behind, and were approaching the Zaïre border.

"In fact, he was trying to dope out our exact position when some rebs *did* start shooting at us, *and* hit the rotor, by God. By the time Rivera got the chopper under control, we didn't have a clue where we were. The radio had taken a couple of slugs, too, and it was too dark to pick up any landmarks. We were limping along, losing altitude fast, when we saw a campfire to the north. We homed on that. We didn't realize we were so near the border, though, so when I saw you and the bush buggy, I figured—"

Griggs nodded. "Yes, you told me about that."

"Anyway, you can see why I need that money now. The alarm is out. And no matter what happens, they'll never believe I didn't plan it all from the beginning."

"That's for certain," he affirmed. "If your outfit's radar picked up the chopper overflying the Brigade and heading for Zaïre . . ."

She drew her finger across her throat. "It's up against the wall for me, Griggs. On the other hand, with the money. . . ." Her eyes made a silent appeal.

Griggs sighed. He switched off the engine and climbed down. From the scabbard riveted to the side of the Rover chassis he unsheathed his machete and threaded his hand through the leather loop. The carbine he passed to Consuela. "I'm only going along to show you it can't be done. We'll have to hack a trail every inch of the way. In jungle like this, you can spit farther than we can travel in a week."

"Somebody or something took a helicopter in there. Where a helicopter can go, we can go," she said reasonably. "We can move a lot faster than whoever's lugging that helicopter around on their back."

Griggs was not so sure. What she said made sense, certainly. But he'd discovered long ago that the *senses*, not sense, were the test of reality in black Africa. And his sixth sense, fine-tuned during the past three years to receive intimations on wavelengths beyond civilized ken, cried out to him to stay away from this particular stretch of jungle. It had always repelled him, for no very good reason, and never was the repulsion stronger than it was now.

But how could he explain this to Consuela? Having demonstrated the night before that he was all man (or so she had assured him, with many a maidenly moan), he was loathe to shatter the illusion by fearing to venture onto a trail along which a helicopter had somehow passed.

He waded into the underbrush. From here on, it would be one step forward, two steps back. He'd have to hack out a path ahead as far as his machete arm would reach, chop the creepers, sword grass, and thistles away from his right leg, take a step forward, repeat the process for his left leg, and then begin all over again. Patches of similarly dense jungle abounded in various parts of the Magenda territory. Sometimes he and his mates had spent weeks surveying an impenetrable four or five square kilometers, only to see it blend into typical tropical rain forest, whose floor was as devoid of fallen leaves and rotten logs as if it had been swept clean, as indeed it was by the multitude of insects, fungi, and bacteria which constantly devoured the fallen debris for their sustenance, eliminating in turn their own wastes to enrich the thin jungle soil in an endless cycle of growth, decay, and regeneration.

He had been slashing at the undergrowth for only two or three minutes, and was just starting to work up a good sweat when suddenly, to his surprise, he was through. It was as if he had sliced through a gossamer but opaque curtain of green. He stepped out onto a trail worn smooth on the jungle floor. It paralleled the margin of the jungle, and was in fact only three or four meters from it at any point which he could see, before it dissolved in the obscurity of the jungle twilight. For here the sunlight was all but extinguished by the dense triple canopy of foliage of trees that soared upwards of eighty meters. He stepped over to the nearest giant, and hacked a blaze the breadth of his palm on its trunk.

"We'll make our trail as we go," he said. He looked to the right. That way led to the point of the dagger spur around which they'd driven to reach this spot, which must be about opposite his camp on the other side. Instinct told him they wouldn't find what they sought in that direction. "This way," he directed. "Hand me my gun. And keep your eyes open."

Griggs started down the trail. It curved gently toward the interior of the jungle, ever deeper into the shadows. Every ten paces or so, he slashed a rasher of bark from the nearest tree, leaving an easily visible mark. Behind him Consuela labored in the early morning heat, which conspired with the moisture-saturated air exhaled by transpiring plant life to produce discomfort like that of a steamship's engine room in August. Neither spoke until, a few minutes after they found the trail, it divided. They paused.

"Which way?" Griggs asked.

"You decide."

"It's your helicopter," he reminded her.

"It's your jungle."

"Well, Connie, if it's left to me, we go back. Haven't you noticed it yet?"

"Noticed what?"

"The jungle. It's dead. No mosquitoes, no flies, no patter of little animal feet, no birds, no mating cries. Jungles are full of noise, Connie. This one is like a tomb. I don't like it."

"Oh, come on, Griggs. The jungle isn't dead. The existence of this trail proves that."

"And that's another thing. This is Magenda territory, and I know every foot of it. But none of them comes near this place. So—who made the trail?"

Consuela tossed her head impatiently and stalked off along the fork to the left, leaving Griggs no option but to follow.

"Why don't you be reasonable, Connie?" he called after her. "How the hell could a helicopter, even taken to pieces, ever pass through here? The trail's less than a meter wide."

She didn't reply.

He felt like kicking her butt. But suddenly her butt wasn't there. It was disappearing around a bend in the trail some distance ahead, moving in high gear, leaving in its wake a tremulous scream of sheer terror. He ran after her, but almost immediately tripped over a root and sprawled headlong. He struggled to his feet and limped after her. For a big woman, she moved fast, and fear had lent her wings.

Her flight and his hot pursuit had taken them past a number of bifurcations in the trail, but Griggs had scarcely noticed. He finally caught up with her and wrapped her in a strong and comforting embrace.

"What the hell happened back there?" he demanded, when she stopped shaking enough to reply.

"*Serpiente*! . . . A huge black snake . . . as thick as your. . . . Ugh! I just couldn't—" She couldn't finish. She pulled his arms tightly about her, shuddering convulsively, and buried her head in his shoulder. "Get me out of here, Griggs."

"You betcha. . . ."

It was late afternoon before he admitted to himself that he had made a promise he could not keep. They were fagged out and starved. And thirsty—the full canteen she carried on her belt had been empty since noon. And lost.

He'd tried to remember how they'd come, and carefully retraced their steps. But each fork in the trail looked much like the others, and though they had gone

back and forth dozens of times, trying alternative
routes, they became ever more irretrievably lost. Not
once did they encounter a tree with the blaze mark
which would have been a signpost to salvation.

As darkness closed in, a breath of air stirred in the
still forest. Griggs grabbed Consuela's arm. By now,
she had regained her former poise, but his hand on
hers brought the apprehension flooding back.

"What is it?"

He sniffed, like a bloodhound onto a scent. He
turned about to face the way they had just come.
"Can't you smell it?" he whispered.

She did: the acrid odor of formic acid. And she realized with sudden panic that it was growing stronger.
Her hand instinctively unbuttoned the flap of the holster and closed around the reassuring knurled butt of
the .45-caliber automatic. Her eyes searched the
shadows.

She saw them first. "Griggs—*look*!"

Two abreast down the narrow trail they came, horribly elongated, unbelievably emaciated beings. They
looked somewhat like year-old babies stretched at the
torso like taffy to a height of some seven feet. Their
skins were bone white and their cylindrical bodies no
bigger around than her thigh, except at the waist,
which she could almost have encircled with one hand.
Most of their hairless bodies, fully three-quarters their
entire height, was torso, with short arms, even shorter
legs and tiny feet that made them waddle like ducks—
a few short, rapid steps, pause, then a few more steps.
As they darted forward, their upper bodies would sway
backward, and as perilously forward as they suddenly
stopped, and oscillated once or twice as they regained
their balance, before darting forward again. The whole
performance reminded Griggs of a London double-
decker bus in heavy traffic, or an American on camel-
back, and would have been hilarious, if the creatures'
awkward gait had not been in their own direction.
They had small, round, unfinished heads, with big sau-
cerlike staring eyes, long thin noses, and tiny ears, as
delicate as rose petals. But the most hideous feature

was their mouths: the pencil-thin semicircular mouths of so many Smiley-buttons, bent in identical, permanent, fatuous grins.

The things didn't look like men, but at least they bled red, and died, as they waddled down the trail, grinning like demented idiots, into the fusillade which Griggs and Consuela immediately—automatically— loosed upon them.

They died quickly and copiously. Each .45-caliber slug that roared from the muzzle of Consuela's pistol ploughed through three or four, tearing out big chunks of white flesh, gouts of red blood pulsing from the wounds. The victims were dead before they fell, like saplings in the wind, to earth, still grinning. Griggs fired as fast as he could load his rifle.

Soon a pile of bodies choked the trail, while those behind mounted the corpses of the dead to be slain in their turn. The two grim warriors soon ran out of ammunition and eventually, having turned their firearms into bludgeons to carry on the carnage, their strength. Weary with crushing skulls and rib cages, which snapped like the stems of sherry glasses, so weary at last that they could no longer lift their leaden arms, they let them fall to their sides.

Consuela closed her eyes and slumped against Griggs. He turned away his head as the grinning things engulfed them, and they were drowned in a sea of soft little baby hands.

5

Griggs felt he was suffocating, so overpowering was the stench of formic acid emanating from the soft, babylike bodies that enveloped him. Then he was hoisted aloft in a cocoon of gentle hands, each gripping him in a feathery, hardly perceived embrace, yet cumulatively rendering him immobile, a Gulliver wrapped in bread dough. He was borne along in swansdown captivity by what seemed to be a kind of conga line, which shuffled forward five steps, hesitated, then took five more quick steps before pausing once again.

The sensation, once he got used to it, was not unpleasant. True, he could see nothing but the faint outline of leafy branches just above him in the obscurity of the jungle, though remarkably enough no more than a hundred meters away, on the savanna, twilight would only now be succeeding day. But if he could see nothing, the abrupt tilt of his body told him he was being carried downhill. Or rather, down a sloping tunnel, for his voice reverberated from a low ceiling when, for the tenth time, he called out to Consuela and, for the tenth time, was answered by silence.

He fought against it, but the rhythmical movement of his bearers, compounded by physical and psychic fatigue, conquered his will to remain awake and alert, and he fell into a shallow slumber. It was the uneasy sleep of the bone-weary traveler, and it was filled with grotesque and frightening dreams.

After what seemed like hours, the cessation of movement roused him. Rude earth rather than velvet hands now sustained him. The stink of alien bodies had disappeared, and in its place was a fragrance of intoxicating beauty. In that transitional realm between sleep and wakefulness, Griggs decided the fragrance must belong to the world of dreams. Certainly the music that accompanied it did. It was a Bach cantata—number 32—which he knew well. It opened with the oboe passage which, as a graduate student, he had played as soloist with the university symphony orchestra and chorale. But the sound of the oboe jostled the memory of the night before, and he asked himself how he could be hearing Bach in the middle of the African jungle. And something else jarred: though the pitch of the voices and instruments was impeccable, and their timing mathematically precise, the dynamics were terrible. Every note, every instrument and voice, was as loud as the next, a series of tones innocent of phrasing or accent. It was as though the bars had been entirely dropped from music played on a synthesizer with the volume control jammed on high gain. This was music defined as organized noise, but to Griggs, it was grotesque—music played by idiots, full of sound and fury, signifying what, he could not guess.

Seized by a sudden disquiet, he opened his eyes and sat up.

He wished he hadn't. . . .

Staring directly into his eyes, not more than five meters away, was a female. Her kinship to the weird beings which had captured him was unmistakable: the same round head, the same long thin missionary's nose, smooth white skin, and rose petal ears. There the resemblance ended. Instead of vacant pink-rimmed eyes, hers were so deep-set and intense that he could not be sure of their color, save that they were dark, and glowed with a luminous intelligence. Her mouth was that of a duchess just offered Coca-Cola at the hunt club breakfast: hard, thin, and disdainful. Her long, dirty white hair was parted in the middle, and cascaded over narrow shoulders like an unraveled floor mat. It flowed down over flattened breasts sagging with years and spread across the padded black dais on which she reclined like an exhausted Lady Buddha. She had no arms.

All this Griggs noted in detail afterward, but what immediately filled his field of vision was a monstrous, mountainous white belly, a gigantic spherical mound of tight white flesh to which, almost as Nature's afterthought, were appended vestigial legs and feet, limp and boneless as if transplanted from a rag doll. Their only apparent function was to frame an incongruously small sexual organ covered with a sparse, scraggly patch of white hair. If heroic human proportions of head to body as laid down by classical artists were, as Griggs recalled, one-to-eight, then this female was the grandmother of all heroines, for her belly alone must have been forty or fifty times the size of her head. It reminded him of a Hortonsphere, one of those immense spherical gas storage tanks at oil refineries, for it was so big he had to look twice to take it all in.

Her appearance was so startling, so completely beyond Griggs' experience and imagination that, for the moment, he could only gape, like a taxpayer confronted with a refund check. Only as his eyes reluctantly became accustomed to the sight, as though he had stepped from the bright sunlight into a darkened room, did he perceive what else the chamber held.

It was a large, roughly rectangular room, as big as the nave of a cathedral. The ceiling was high, lost to the room's sole source of illumination, a pink glow that seemed to issue from the base of the walls. The dark walls themselves were irregular, unfinished and without decoration. Of furnishings there were none except the dais, which appeared to be a fine black sponge, on which the grotesque being reclined. But she was not alone. To one side stood some 150 individuals who could have been distant cousins to those who had captured him. They had barrel chests placed on infants' legs, and mouths with almost human lips instead of semicircular slits like the others. The cousins came in all sizes. The shortest was barely waist high, while the tallest towered more than a meter above him. And those almost-human lips were moving, and what came from between them were the orchestral and choral sounds of the Bach cantata.

The player-piano music, the delicious fragrance, the unbelievable female staring into his eyes—it was all crazy. Where the hell am I? Griggs asked himself in sudden panic.

In the realm of the Formigans.

Griggs started. He hadn't spoken. And he was sure no one else had. Yet his unspoken question had been heard, and answered. By whom?

By JEH, Queen of the Formigans.

He squinted at the unmoving lips. But how?

In the manner of the Formigans, which is not of your world.

Griggs turned away, his mind in turmoil. Aside from a mouth as dry as sawdust, a ringing in the ears, and sweaty palms, he felt perfectly normal. He realized he should be terrified. Any mortal in his position would be. But though a mortal, he was also a scientist. And the scientist, his excitement kindled by the prospect of earth-shaking revelations, took charge. Now look, Griggs the scientist said to Griggs the quaking mortal, kindly be terrified some other time. Right now, I've got work to do. I've stumbled upon a completely new species whose existence has never even been suspected. Its morphology seems primitive, but its means of communication surpasses any known to mankind. I may have made the greatest single scientific discovery of all time. An eyewitness description of these beings will put Maynard Griggs right up there with Charles Darwin. It's the chance of a lifetime and—get this straight, you quaking coward—you're not going to muff it . . . And speaking of muff, what the hell could have happened to Consuela? He looked up expectantly.

A white silence.

That's funny, Griggs thought. She didn't catch the question.

What question?

Where's Consuela?

The female? She is near.

Is she . . . alive?

Yes.

Is she—has she been hurt?

No.

Where is she?

Near.

And safe, you say?

Yes.

Can I see her?

Yes.

He relaxed a little. So long as she was safe, she could wait. Meanwhile, he had questions. He looked over at the chorus. Why are those people singing?

No reply.

He pointed, his eyes following his finger. "Who's that singing?" he asked aloud.

No reply.

He looked back at Queen JEH. Come on—who's singing?

My sons.

Griggs cast his eyes heavenward with the thrill of discovery. So, Queen JEH was not all-knowing, after all. True, she could read his thoughts and project her own into his consciousness, but only when their eyes touched. To be alone with his thoughts, he simply had to disengage his gaze. He turned back.

Who brought me here?

My sons.

You've got zillions of 'em, he thought wryly.

Yes.

Well, why did they bring me here?

No answer formed in Griggs' mind. He waited.

Why?

The wall of silence remained unbreached. Griggs experienced another surge of optimism. If her method of communication was extrasensory, even supernatural, far superior to that of civilized beings, at least her logical processes were not. She could understand and reply to such questions as who, where and what, but *why*—involving causality and consequence—was apparently an alien concept. That put her mental equipment on a plane below that of humankind. Observation and communication of facts were within her capability; reason was beyond it, as would be planning—the manipulation of hypothetical cause and effect. Deceit being a form of planning, the contrivance of an effect based on false premises, she would also therefore be incapable of lying. Thus, reasoned Griggs, who was a better anthropologist than logician, whatever she told him must be the absolute truth, so far as she knew it. The thought was very reassuring. There was just one thing, though. . . .

What do you know about what happened—up there?

Everything.

Are you—ah—angry because I defended myself?

Anger is unknown to Formigans.

What do you intend doing with me?

Silence.

Griggs smiled inwardly. Another point for the home team. That thought, designed to confirm his assumption that prevision—and therefore planning—was beyond her, had been answered: it was. For the Formigans, the future did not exist.

Can I go if I wish, then?

You can go.

And Consuela?

And the female.

When?

At a moment of your choosing.

Am I in any danger here?

Is the tree endangered by the orchid?

Griggs by now felt relaxed enough to grin, remembering how easily he had dispatched the Formigans. For a moment, he not only forgot that the parasitic Orchidaceae comprise the largest—and therefore most successful—of all plant families, with more than 30,-000 species, but that in the end the Formigans had made him prisoner.

Do you know who I am?

What you know, I know.

Oh, yeah? thought Griggs, feeling more cocky by the

minute. Who's the best pro football quarterback of all time?

There was no reply.

Griggs snorted. Some times he considered John Unitas the best, at other times he thought Fran Tarkenton took the palm, but old ugly here couldn't pull even one of their names out from under his hat. It didn't occur to him that he didn't know the answer to his question, himself.

Griggs breathed easier. He was obviously in control. She said he could leave anytime he wanted, and he believed her. But the knowledge that he could obviated any immediate necessity to do so. Now that his retreat was secure, he must capitalize on his discovery of the Formigans by wringing out of them every scrap of information about their origins and way of life. And Griggs thought he knew a way to accomplish this purpose.

He had established that Queen JEH could penetrate his mind by the intermediation of their eyes. But the *questions* he had asked were of his own volition. And she had answered them all, every single one, save those dealing with future or conditional events. But hell, even humans had trouble with those. Furthermore, apparently she spoke the truth, so far as she knew it. What if, he asked himself, her nature was such that she *had* to respond? What if a response to questions was as automatic to the Formigan Queen JEH as light reflected from a mirror? And why not? After all, she was captive of her own grotesque body. She could be equally in thrall to his questions. If so, the answer to them all was here, looking at him.

There was one way to find out.

Tell me about the Formigans, Queen JEH.

And, by God, she did . . .

6

The Formigans were an ancient people, a race of darkness, already many rains old when the first outlander came. He was a black man, and ever after, black men were a commonplace among the Formigans. White men appeared less often. The earliest were two who had escaped their abode, a strange abode which they said fled from the wind across the waters, from a place far distant. They were of the tribe of the Phoenicus, called themselves Carthaginians, and served a master named Hanno, who was seeking to journey to the very edge of the Earth. The two men remained. Down the ages, others came questing: Greeks for trade, Arabs for converts to their new religion, Portuguese priests for a certain King Prester John, Dutchmen for slaves, Frenchmen in black gowns for black souls, Belgians for the fruits of the inner Earth, Englishmen for the inedible skins of edible animals, which they disdained to eat. None of these did the Formigans possess, yet the outlanders stayed.

Why? Griggs asked the question automatically, before he realized its futility. He rephrased it: was there something in the land of the Formigans they had not found elsewhere?

Queen JEH told him: there was peace, and there was plenty. The outlanders spoke of sufferings—of cold and heat, of hunger and thirst. These things did not exist here, and their absence reassured the outlanders. Nor were there beasts and men here to prey upon them. Nor the uncertainty as to what the next moment would bring, for this was foreordained.

Sounds like a Russian paradise, said Griggs to himself.

Perhaps. Outlanders have spoken of Russians. But none have come.

Give them time. Just now they're busy making the rest of Africa a paradise.

If they are to come, they will come. All is predestined.

Good and bad, like love and anger, Griggs learned, didn't exist among the Formigans. Things were the way they were. The outlanders told of uncertainties, misunderstandings, conflicts, disbelief, deception, disloyalty, irresolution, cowardice, and other affections. These had no reality in the Formigan world, where all was ordered by one supreme animate nature—that of the queen . . .

The queen was at the apex of the Formigan world. The princes, whose function was minimal and transitory, were at the bottom. They were members of a sheltered group whose life was to await death—the death of the reigning queen. When her end was imminent, the princelings were given a special food. A metamorphosis thereupon took place: a differentiation of the sexes, in the proportion of one prince for every seven princesses. Both sexes quickly developed to maturity, and copulation followed. The princes died immediately afterward, presumably, Griggs speculated, from ecstasy. The first litter of offspring to appear were infant princelings. When they were assured of healthy survival, their mother became queen; all the other princesses followed the princes into oblivion, perhaps from chagrin.

Other castes maintained the continuity of the community. Long ago, many rains in the past, a numerous and powerful warrior caste battled the *ogulg*, the heavy-scaled burrowing beast that shared the nether world with them and preyed on Formigan flesh. War had raged for generations. The warrior's smell was their only weapon against the *ogulg*. But it was a powerful one, for it enfeebled and usually killed the enemy which chose to fight rather than flee. When the last *ogulg* had been driven away, the Formigans found themselves in sole possession of the underground realm. The warriors, lacking an enemy to stimulate their natural defenses, in time lost their power to kill: the scent became attenuated, feared but not fatal. They then became the *guards* of the forest, warning off the great cats, wart hogs, snakes, and other enemies by the collective repellency of their odor. These were the Formigans Griggs and Consuela had encountered.

The scent of the *guards* usually sufficed to make all living creatures run for their lives, but when their atavistic instincts became aroused by a natural enemy standing its ground, the *guards* did not hesitate to attack, and by mere weight of numbers invariably prevailed. But their function was pacific: to clear the forest of predators so the *gleaners* could harvest without molestation Formigan food bases such as leaves, twigs, thistles, grasses, dead logs and branches, small dead animals, and bird droppings. The total removal of this jungle debris accounted for the eerily and unnaturally clean condition of the jungle floor Griggs had observed, and the absence of visible animal life.

The overall, long-term effect of the removal of the detritus, though perhaps esthetically appealing to the civilized eye, was far from benign, for it starved the parasites and bacteria that would normally have decomposed the organic material into its constituent nutrient chemicals, which rain returned to the thin and frail jungle soil. The result was a progressive impoverishment of the forest ecosphere. One day it would collapse. The thousands of interdependent plant species, in their turn starved into debility, would quickly succumb to whichever of nature's crises—fire, drought, or pestilence—came along first. Brown desert would succeed green jungle. This had already happened in areas surrounding the strip of jungle beneath which the Formigans now lived, and Griggs wondered whether they had been responsible for the catastrophic change in the Zaïrian and Angolan landscapes over the course of centuries.

That their way of life was predatory—though their prey was dead organic matter that littered the jungle floor—was of no concern to the Formigans, who could not in any case appreciate such philosophical niceties. They went on blindly destroying the jungle that provided them sustenance, and wondered not that it was replaced in time by the sere savanna which supported only acacia trees, scrub grasses, a sparse population of wild game, and the tse-tse fly. It was the only way of life they knew, and how could they guess that the jungle was not eternally renewable, and did not stretch out to infinity?

So the *gleaners* collected the debris of the forest as they had done for thousands of years, and segregated it in separate dark chambers underground. In each chamber *planters* impregnated the dead material with the various species of fungi the Formigans needed to support the community. How many species of fungi they raised Griggs would never be able to compute, but they were certainly a generous representation of the 50,-000-odd fungi identified by mycologists—plus some that hadn't been—and their uses embraced every conceivable need of the primitive society.

Mushrooms and truffles of an infinite variety were the staple foods of the Formigans. All were eaten raw: cooking was unknown to them. Field mushrooms, blewits, cep, morel, shaggy parasol, fairy-ring champignon and other varieties well-known to the civilized world abounded. But specialized species of fungi and yeasts, besides providing the carbohydrates and minerals needed to sustain the higher forms of life—Darwin reported that the Yaghans of Tierra del Fuego subsisted largely on a single species of fungus—also had achieved such biological sophistication that they synthesized protein indistinguishable in taste, Griggs would find, from *steak tartare*.

The *indki,* globular fungus, as large as a golf ball, contained pure water, so far as Griggs could determine. It obviously sucked the water out of the atmosphere itself, for the chambers in which it was cultivated were extraordinarily dry, and the ventilation system of the underground passages passed air through the areas where this particular fungus was grown. In Griggs' view, the mechanism was apparently a refinement of the familiar fungus phenomenon—the absorption of atmospheric moisture by the surface of the living mycelium, diffusing through the hyphal wall into the protoplasm of the cell, which it swelled to fantastic proportions. Alternatively, it may have been a variety of the *Tremella*, whose wall expands in the presence of water and in its terrestrial forms becomes gelatinized, although the Formigan *indki's* contents remained clear and liquid. The *indki* came in an assortment of soft pastel pinks. The outer skin of the fungus, when chewed, imparted a pleasant, subtle flavor to the water it contained, but flavorless water was obtained merely by spitting out the skin unchewed.

A lesser number of algae, cultivated in icy underground cavern waters far beneath the surface, also provided basic nutrients required by the Formigans. A freshwater relative of the *Porphyra*, rich in protein and vitamins B and C, was consumed in quantity, though hardly in the manner of the Welsh, who fry the *Porphyra umbilicalis* with a coating of oatmeal—and eat it for breakfast.

A vast collection of molds, slimes, mildews, and giant spores performed functions for which civilized man relied on human skills and complicated machinery. For example, the Formigans excavated their chambers and tunnels by means of a remarkable strain of the hydrophilic *indki*, one which multiplied so exuberantly that its spores would burst and send out flagellate stalks which efficiently sucked up whatever moisture the soil harbored. Within seconds the stalks would drill an arm's length below the soil's surface, riddling it with thousands of tiny tendrils, which then funneled the condensed moisture back to the swelling cell body. When the cell nucleus became bloated it entered the reproductive stage, spontaneously separating itself from the flagella and dropping off the wall to which it was attached. The flagella, now but empty, thin-walled tubes, were all that held the brittle soil together. As they dried and shriveled, the soil became geostatically unstable. A sharp blow caused the frangible soil to collapse, whereupon it was only necessary to haul it away. This fungal bulldozer the Formigans called *emusdor*.

Rodsume was a slime mold that almost perfectly complemented the spore *emusdor*. It was quiescent while desiccated, and it was therefore stored when not needed in one of the arid finger caverns where the water fungus, the *indki*, was produced. When a partition, bridge, or other permanent structure had to be constructed, however, a bit of *rodsume*—half a teaspoonful would suffice—was smeared at the base of the projected addition. Water from punctured *indki* was poured on it. This stimulated the slime to furious germination through the formation of swarm cells. These new cells, somewhat like the tendrils of the *emusdor*, spread out from the mother cell with wriggling flagella, but with a significant difference: where the *emusdor* radiated from their source and kept their individual identity, the *rodsume* flagella intertwined in mad confusion, like a can of agitated worms. Where one touched another, an inseparable bond was formed. Growth did not cease there, however, but continued outward from the basal cell in a proliferating network.

Up to this point, the *rodsume* was not unlike many common slime molds, but now its utility as a building material became apparent. As it grew it could, being moist, be shaped. This was done by the Formigans according to the purpose to which it was to be put—a partition would be patted into its predetermined configuration as it rose vertically from the floor, a pillar pressed into a smooth cylinder, an arch formed from both ends, tapering toward the join in the center. The continued growth of the ends of the slime mold hyphae, or filaments, demanded a steady provision of water. This came from the base of each tendril of the mold. It was rather as if a long line of total abstainers passed along a whiskey-filled bucket, each one drinking a half pint neat before he handed it to the next in line. Before the bucket reached the end of the line, those at the beginning would be stiff. That—literally—happened to the *rodsume*: as water continued to be applied to the base of the slime mold, those mother cells became engorged, triggering a chemical reaction which caused a progressive calcification to set in. Like the calcareous shells of dying polyps of a growing coral reef, they hardened to the consistency of granite.

Still another fungus, which was strongly phosphorescent, lighted the Formigans' tunnels and chambers, although in some of the caverns, where certain specialized fungi demanding total darkness were grown, it was excluded. By a careful control of nutrients, the light level was kept very low, for Formigans were intolerant of intensities humans can easily bear. The color of the phosphorescence depended on the strain of fungus species, and the various specialized chambers were color coded to provide instant orientation by the Formigans, who were as susceptible to navigation error as humans. The Queen's court, for example, was pink. The nursery of the Formigan princelings was pink. The cavern where the *rodsume* slime was cultivated was pink. To the human eye, indeed, the entire Formigan realm was pink. But not to the more discriminating Formigan eye, which could distinguish color gradations considerably less than an angstrom unit apart in the vicinity of 6700Å. By way of nature's compensation, they were unable to discriminate between say, green and purple, elsewhere in the visible spectrum.

In addition to the Queen, *guards* and *gleaners*, there were a number of other castes of Formigans, each distinguished by unique physical attributes. The *planters*, for instance, in place of fingers had long, feathery appendages which were specialized for the impregnation of the materials brought down from the jungle above, distributing spores and slimes of the hundreds of varieties of fungus according to the immediate needs of the community.

The *courtiers* were responsible for the feeding of the Queen, and delivering the young, which were turned over at birth to the *guardians*. Of the latter there were two classes: the superior cared for the princelings, kept them strictly segregated from the other Formigans, and fed them special foods, while the larger but inferior subclass nurtured all other castes to maturity.

Healers tended the sick and wounded, using a range of fungi as medicaments. The green mold *penicillium* was considered by them one of the more common applications to ward off infection, and useful only for minor injuries. They had far better.

The *memorialists* were a squat breed of Formigan, with huge heads and tiny, squashed bodies, who sat out their lives in long rows in darkness in special chambers, like cans of beans on a storeroom shelf. The darkness helped them conserve their energies and focus them on the memorization of the events occurring in the Formigan realm down through the thousands of rains, the genealogies of the succession of queens, the thousands of strains of fungi and the special qualities and uses associated with each, and the voluminous recollections of the hundreds of outlanders who had entered the realm of the Formigans in the vastness of time.

Each *memorialist* was the narrowest of specialists. One, for example, commanded the grammatical rules of Latin, a language bequeathed to the Formigans by a Portuguese priest of long ago, with examples he had cited for each. That same *memorialist* happened also to be the reserve repository of another *memorialist's* principal responsibility: hair—hair of the rat, the leopard, the black man, the white man, its uses, occurrence, and everything else about the subject which had been combed from the experience of the community from its beginning, including a great deal of useless fluff as well as interesting stuff they could produce on cue.

Another *memorialist* carried in his mind as complete a lexicon of Latin as the priest could compile, with definitions in both Latin and Greek supplied to the best of the priest's powers of recall, along with Portuguese glosses. This particular *memorialist's* sideline was economic theory, a mishmash of Marx, Ricardo, Keynes, Smith, and Friedman, summoned up from the depths of recollection by various outlanders, to whom it made as little sense as it did to the Formigans.

The *memorialists* filled many chambers, and apprentices sat at the feet of each, learning their voluminous and largely inapplicable secrets, to be transmitted down the generations. The study went on for years, in perfect silence, for they communicated by means the nature of which the Formigans themselves were unable to explain, no more than horse players can explain why sure winners so often finish out of the money.

And then there were the *minstrels*.

Griggs glanced toward the barrel-chested crew with quasi-human lips which, since the silent colloquy between him and Queen JEH began, had uttered no sound, but stood sheeplike, unmoving, unaware of each other's presence, like commuters waiting for the 7:23 out of Bridgeport.

Yes, they are my minstrels.

You must like music.

Like? That word does not exist for Formigans.

Then why do they sing?

Silence.

Sorry, said Griggs, and rephrased the question. What is their function?

They sing the music of ten thousand rains . . .

The minstrels were both the *memorialists* of music and its performers. Their history went back to the origin of the Formigan species. During the nuptial embrace, the prince deposited within the queen spermatozoa sufficient to fertilize the innumerable ova she produced. The spermatozoa were released by the queen's seminal vesicle, however, only in response to a rhythmic stroking of her body by the attendants, accompanied by a monotonal chant. This had been the custom far beyond memory, and had produced a modest but stable population. Eventually, and unaccountably, the Formigan death rate began to exceed the birth rate, and it seemed that the race was shrinking toward extinction.

Rescue came by accident. One of the two Carthaginians, the first white man to appear, was given to singing, and it was observed that—presumably as a result—the fecundity of the queen was enormously enhanced. The sailor's small stock of sea chanties was forthwith committed to memory by the attendants, and the population shot back up, considerably beyond its former level. Yet the long-range effect was the same: the potency of the music, too, diminished with time and repetition.

With each new visitor the process was the same. Any new music had, for a period, the effect of accelerating the growth of the Formigan population. The effect was reinforced by the evolution of the *minstrel* caste, which had long since ceased to stroke the queen's body and now concentrated solely on singing. True to the Formigans' predelection for genetic specialization, the *minstrels* could individually sing through the range of only one note apiece, although they were capable of producing each note in a tremendous variety of acoustic patterns—as an organ, violin, human voice, tambourine, even snare drums. Unfortunately, they were not blessed with dynamic range: every note was delivered at the same amplitude as every other. Their impeccable sense of time, however, at least allowed these notes to be delivered in smooth sequence so that few listeners could detect any discontinuity. Griggs, at first astonished, remembered that the Swingles Singers had done much the same thing, imitating orchestral renditions with uncanny fidelity, although each member of the ensemble carried a whole melodic line instead of chopping it up into its component notes, as did the Formigans.

Yet the Formigans were themselves incapable of composing any original music, and instead of invention relied on repetition, performing their complete repertoire through to the end, only to begin it again from the start. Some music—*The Trojans* of Berlioz, for example—heard on a tiny black box brought by a Belgian priest in a not-too-distant time, had produced a frenzy of fertility, yet it too eventually petered out. By now, all known music had been repeated thousands of times. It had become banal, wearisome and uninspiring—music by Muzak. And the Formigan population, though incessantly hectored by the sound of music, was once again slipping backward.

For three rains past, no new litters had been conceived. The music had lost its effect. But his coming had saved the Formigans.

"Me?" Griggs said, aloud. "How?"

Queen JEH detached her eyes from his. They looked past him.

Griggs turned. A Formigan, one of those with the grin, was bobbing forward in his little conga shuffle. In his baby-soft hands he bore Griggs' oboe. He handed it to Griggs and danced away.

You will play.

"I will?"

Yes. You want to play. Queen JEH's eyes bored into his. Her gross body lay like a beached whale upon the dais, obscene in its obesity, totally repulsive in its fish-belly whiteness. Yet the delicate fragrance that wafted his way imprisoned his other senses, and he realized that, despite the impression of his eyes, he was not unfavorably disposed toward Queen JEH. That his feeling was to a large extent influenced by his hope of learning the secrets of this amazing race of semihumans and transmitting them to his own world to his everlasting celebrity, he was not prepared to admit even to himself.

He looked down at the instrument he held, and fingered the familiar keys.

"Well, I guess maybe I—" he had started to say, when a hysterical scream ripped through his utterance. The cry came from nearby. The voice was Consuela's.

7

The royal chamber had but one entrance, a low-ceilinged passage behind him, and Griggs was off and running as Consuela's cry still echoed from it. Blocking the entrance were scores of Formigans, but he plowed through them like a bull through tall grass, and sped on at a dead run down the dim tunnel.

Like those he had observed while being carried down into Queen JEH's realm, the tunnel was low and narrow: the walls were scarcely beyond the reach of his outstretched arms, and he could brush the ceiling with his fingertips. The illumination, fainter than that of the royal chamber, was a pale pink, and came from low luminous strips that lined both sides of the passageway. Otherwise, the surfaces of the tunnel were a uniform smooth blue-black.

He had run about the length of a football field when the tunnel veered off to the left, then abruptly broadened out to become a room only slightly less cavernous than the one he had just left. It too was softly illuminated by luminous strips of pink fungus which ran around its periphery. At the far end of the room, silhouetted against the dim light, was a mass of Formigans from which a puzzling sort of sound—part outrage, part incredulity, part hysterical cackle—reverberated. Griggs was across the room in a bound, scattering Formigans as if they were chaff in a high wind.

There, lying on her back, completely nude, was Consuela, pressed down by two score dainty white hands. Atop her was a Formigan of a breed Griggs had not seen. His torso was vibrating with the rapidity of a tattoo needle, causing his diminutive legs and feet to jiggle about in midair in a Punch-and-Judy pantomime. Caressing Consuela's breasts were appendages which resembled feather dusters or wings more than hands. He was the busiest Formigan Griggs had yet observed and he was, predictably, grinning.

Griggs wasn't. He reached down, grabbed the Formigan by the neck, and flung him halfway across the room, bowling over three or four of his comrades. They were seemingly unoffended. Even the thwarted lover rose shakily and, still grinning, did his little conga-step straight back to his place aboard Consuela. Griggs smashed him with the oboe he discovered he was still carrying. The Formigan's spindly arm snapped like dry spaghetti. So did the oboe. Griggs cast it aside and energetically dispersed those who pinioned Consuela with a flurry of rib-shattering kicks and punches in the Smiley-grins and goggling eyes. The victims who weren't felled scuttled away to a safe distance, there to grin idiotically at their aggressor. But none moved in. Griggs measured them with his eyes, decided they were no immediate menace, and gave his attention to Consuela.

She sat up, shaking. "God damn. God *damn*!" she said over and over, pounding her fist into her open palm.

"Okay, take it easy, Connie," Griggs whispered, kneeling beside her and taking her in his arms.

She giggled inanely.

"Come on—snap out of it!"

She gently disengaged his arms and looked up into his eyes. "What's this—the new Griggs?" she asked, with mock solemnity. "Solace for the fallen woman?"

"Did they hurt you?" He cursed himself for his obvious stupidity. Of course rape hurt. He moved to get up. "I think I'd better kill a few of them miserable sonsofbitches," he grated.

Consuela held him back. "You'll do nothing of the kind."

"Huh?"

"Leave them alone, I said."

"The hell I will. They *were* raping you, weren't they?"

"Well, yes—I guess you could call it that."

"Well, what would *you* call it?"

"Oh, I don't know—pathetic, maybe."

"Tearing your insides to pieces—you call that pathetic?"

Consuela laid a cool hand on his cheek. "You are a lovely man, did you know that? A sentimentalist of the old school. Now, let me see if I can describe it to you, Griggs." She bit her lip, frowning in concentration. Finally she smiled. "Yes—hummingbirds."

"What?"

"Exactly. It was like being assaulted by a flock of hummingbirds."

"You're around the bend, Connie."

"Not me. Why do you think I was laughing?"

"That was laughing?" Well, maybe it was, now that he thought about it. Hysteria covered a lot of emotions.

"Of course. Wouldn't you laugh, if somebody was tickling your crotch with a feather?"

"Jesus!" He'd never understand women. He hardly imagined that the first rape victim he'd ever had to deal with would find the experience hilarious. But she definitely wasn't disturbed.

Neither were the Formigans, goggling at the two of them, grinning like apes.

"Put your clothes on," Griggs snapped, gathering them up while keeping an eye on the spectators. "We're getting out of here."

She dressed quickly and buckled on the web belt with its now-empty holster. "How?"

Griggs regarded her oddly. "What did I say just then?"

"You said we're getting out of here. Why?"

Griggs stroked his chin. "That's what I thought I said."

"Well, why not? We *are* getting out of here, aren't we?"

"You bet your ass, kiddo. But the funny thing is,

when I took off out of the royal chamber a minute ago,
I had every intention of—"

"Out of *what*?"

"The royal . . . I guess I'd better explain a few
things."

He led her past the mob of Formigans, toward the
tunnel leading to Queen JEH's chamber, prepared to
bash the first to bar their way, almost wishing the creatures would so he could hear the soothing crackle of
Formigan bone. "Listen, Connie, you'd better prepare
yourself for a shock. In fact, several . . ."

He described the Formigan ruler and their wordless
colloquy in the royal chamber, and gave her a brief
résumé of the gospel according to Queen JEH. "And
strangely enough," he concluded, "when I heard your
scream, I was actually getting to feel pretty much at
ease, and had just about decided to stay awhile."

"Now who's around the bend?"

"Well, why not? The two of us have put quite a
number out of commission, permanently, and they
haven't so much as bruised us. I think they're too
dumb to hurt us. Just think—I could write a book
right now on the observations I've made in the two
hours I've been down here. Give me two days, and the
scientific discoveries I'd come up with would make me
the most celebrated anthropologist on earth. I'd use
Nobel prize citations for Kleenex."

"Then what made you change your mind about stay-
ing?"

"I'm not sure. Something. Maybe just a hunch. But I
can tell you this: any discoveries I make, scientific or
otherwise, are going to be behind a battalion of U.S.
Marines with fixed bayonets. There's something fishy
about this place, and I don't intend to hang around to
find out what it is."

"I'm ready. Let's go."

"We've got to find out how, first. That means we've
got to have another talk with old tumor tummy."

"Do you think she was telling the truth?" Consuela
asked as they reached the entrance to the royal cham-

ber, with a horde of Formigans trailing at a discreet distance.

"About what?"

"About everything. But especially about being able to walk out of here whenever you want to."

"I doubt it. Would they have brought us down here just so we could waltz right out again? Not bloody likely. Still, we'll jolly her along and see what happens. But watch your step. Don't antagonize her. I can always strong-arm her, of course, but first I want to know what she might have up her sleeve."

"Don't worry about me," Consuela assured him. "Diplomacy is my middle name."

Griggs took her hand and led her into the royal chamber before the Queen of the Formigans. He instantly regretted it.

The mutual repulsion of the two females was instantaneous and unmistakable. They glared at each other with the unsheathed hostility of two cats eyeball to eyeball on an alley fence. Neither stirred. Their eyes locked together in the ocular equivalent of war.

"Okay, you big tub of guts," boomed Consuela, unable to restrain her sudden antipathy, "what's the big idea?"

Big idea?

"You can drop the innocent act. You told Griggs that I was all right, that no harm would come to me. Well, sister, harm's all that didn't come. The word is rape."

Rape?

"Shove without love, emission without permission. What that vibrating asparagus stalk was doing to me. Rape."

My son was defending his queen against a usurper.

"Who—*me*?"

You—who would conquer the realm of the Formigans, and be queen in my stead.

Consuela looked helplessly at Griggs. "The old bag's around the bend, too. What do you think's causing all this—air pollution?"

Griggs looked at Queen JEH thoughtfully. What caste is your son the defender of his queen?

My son is a healer.

"*Healer?*" exclaimed an indignant Consuela. "I'm not sick, for Christ sake. And if I was, that animated whisk broom dusting my pelvis wouldn't cure me."

On the contrary, he has done so. The Formigan realm has been spared.

"Spared—spared what?"

Invasion.

"Now, look here," Consuela began, her voice low and ominous, "I've had about enough of you. I didn't invade your stupid realm—I was brought here. And another little thing, I—"

"Hold it, Connie," Griggs broke in. "I think I've got a glimmer."

He faced Queen JEH. When did your sons the scouts first see the female Consuela?

When she emerged from the belly of her mother.

Then who is the female Consuela?

An alien queen. The queen of the sky.

Griggs glanced significantly at Consuela. She shook her head, baffled.

Why has she come?

Silence.

Does she threaten the Formigans?

No longer.

Griggs nodded. And your son the healer eliminated the danger?

Yes. Disaster has been averted.

And what does your son the healer do when he— ah—isn't healing females like Consuela?

He heals the roots and leaves and logs of the forest, so that they may be impregnated with the seed of the Formigans.

Griggs smiled triumphantly. "There's your answer, Connie," he said. "You see, big mama here had you pegged for a rival queen, come to take over the Formigan homeland."

"Me? A queen?" She turned angrily to Queen JEH. "You think if I were a queen I'd be wasting my time in an overgrown termite mound like this? You must be out of your mind. You—"

"Connie," Griggs was saying patiently. "Connie!"

She looked at Griggs.

He said: "If you keep your eyes on me when you talk, she won't know what you're saying. She can't hear—she can only communicate by means of visual signals passing between her eyes and those of another."

"All right, what's this about me being a queen?"

"The helicopter. The Formigans saw it coming in for a landing. Probably the first aircraft they ever saw up close. When it crashed, you climbed out. That makes you the daughter of the helicopter."

"Helicopters don't have daughters," she pointed out sweetly.

"I know that. And you know it. But do the Formigans? I doubt it. All they know is that the beast flies through the air, and makes noise, and gives birth to young—you and the pilot—and it dies. That's a fair approximation of what happens with bird life, in the limited Formigan experience. To them, Connie, the helicopter was animate."

Consuela Millán y Gorgas shook her head. "It doesn't make sense, Griggs. Look—they captured us in the forest. They must have wanted us, for some reason. Well, then, why didn't they capture us when we were out there alone last night? Well, go on—ask her why."

Griggs shook his head. "Forget it. Old Queen JEH's pretty savvy, but ask her why, and it simply doesn't register. Anyway, I think *I* can tell you why."

"I'm listening."

"Well, you see, when a Formigan queen dies, there is an immediate differentiation of the sexes among the princelings. I told you how that works. Then copulation takes place, whereupon the male also dies.

"Now, nothing happened up there last night that would surprise a reasonably intelligent Formigan guard, if such exists. The helicopter—read queen—fell to the ground and died. Though at the time they couldn't of course see you inside the chopper, they later presumed that the two princelings the queen carried, up to that moment identical—the uniforms you wore were after all the same, metamorphosed into male and female. You copulated. Then the male died and you emerged, ready to spawn squadrons of little helicopters. So far, all has accorded with Formigan experience."

"All right," the woman agreed, "but if they saw all this, and made all these deductions, and wanted me, why didn't they take me right then?"

"Because *I* showed up in a Range Rover with the headlights blazing—remember? They're nocturnal. They can't stand strong light. So before they could grab you, I hauled you off in the Rover."

"They had plenty of time to take me at your place."

"I was already doing that," he reminded her, with a lewd smile. "Besides, there was moonlight."

"There was, wasn't there?" Her eyes softened.

"But today, when we went into the jungle, circumstances had changed. Now you were an invader of Queen JEH's territory. You had a belly full of little flying machines. You'd start delivering them, and in short order they'd deliver to you, mother, the Formigan kingdom."

"*Queen*dom."

"Call it realm. That made you an enemy."

"So why didn't they just kill me?"

Griggs shrugged. "Beats me. I guess—wait. . . . Of course! They heard you singing. The old biddy needs music for her own procreative processes, and she knew you could supply it. But if you came down here and started dropping baby-blue helicopters in little booties, she'd be in mortal danger. The answer: your feathered friend."

Consuela looked blank. "You've lost me, Griggs."

"I asked her if you were any danger to the Formigans, and she said, quote, 'No longer.' She said young Feather Fingers, her son, heals the logs and leaves of the forest so they can be planted for food for the Formigans."

"Bullshit."

"Unless I am much mistaken, he can heal that too.

The way I see it, those feather dusters are specialized organs, impregnated with some powerful mold-produced antibiotic which sterilizes everything it touches. It wipes out all the unwanted parasites and bacteria from the animal and vegetable bases on which the Formigans culture their fungi. Once the extraneous microscopic life is eliminated, they can then culture their pure strains without competition."

"Do you mean? . . ."

"I'm afraid so, Mother," Griggs said gravely. "You're not going to hear the pitter-patter of little rotor blades after all."

"Crazy. Everybody's crazy," she muttered. "Well, let's see how it fits," she went on. She turned belligerently on Queen JEH, who had not so much as blinked during the conversation between Consuela and Griggs. "All right, you old bitch, what did you do with my mother?"

What one does with the dead: my sons buried her.

"By God, Griggs," she laughed, delightedly, "you were right! She really thinks that helicopters have . . ." She rounded on Queen JEH. "Buried her—*where*?"

Where she died.

"*Emusdor* and *rodsume*," mused Griggs. "It figures."

"*Now* what are you talking about?"

"Never got around to telling you that, did I? *Emusdor* is sort of a crabgrass among fungi. It sinks its tendrils into soil and sucks out the last drop of moisture, leaving it dry and crumbly. It must work pretty fast. Obviously, when the Formigan scouts saw the 'dead' helicopter 'queen,' they succumbed to conditioned reflex and buried it."

"How?"

"Simple. They'd have applied *emusdor* to the earth beneath the helicopter, forming a shallow depression into which the helicopter would sink. Several applications of the *emusdor* would, I gather, lower the chopper below the surface."

"We didn't see any depression with a helicopter sitting in it," she reminded him.

"That's because after they formed a cavity below ground level, they roofed it over with *rodsume*."

"*Rodsume*." She sighed.

"Exactly. This is a slime which soaks up water and expands like a sponge. It can be shaped while it's growing, but when it dries, it hardens to the consistency of cement. That accounts for the formic acid smell we detected where the chopper crashed: after they roofed it over, they dusted soil from the surrounding area over it as camouflage against carrion eaters like hyenas. Then they went back into the jungle to descend into the grotto from another entrance. We know that for sure, because we followed their tracks."

"Then the helicopter was there all the time, right under our feet?"

"It's the only answer that fits the facts we've got."

"And all I have to do to get my money is dig?"

"Seems so."

She hitched up her belt and squared her shoulders. "How do I get out of here?" she asked Queen JEH.

You don't want to stay among us.

"Truer words were never uttered, sister."

Then sing for me.

"Some other time."

I will wait.

"You may wait a long time, fatso. We chopper queens don't take kindly to abortion. Haven't you ever heard of the 'right to life?' "

No.

"I thought not. Well, no hard feelings—providing you tell me how to get the hell out of here, at once."

My sons will carry you.

"Nothing doing. We'll walk."

As you wish. My sons will show you the way.

"No tricks?"

Tricks?

"Not that I can't take care of myself, mind you. Just show me where to fill my canteen and we'll be off."

"Hey!" Griggs exclaimed.

"What's the matter?"

"Do you realize that we've been down here a couple of hours, at least?"

"Uh—yes, I guess so."

"Aren't you thirsty?"

Consuela licked her lips. "Why, no," she said, surprised.

"Neither am I. Yet we were both dying for a drink by noon—and it must be at least midnight by now." He addressed the thought to Queen JEH.

You drank indki *while you slept.* A wave of fragrance washed over them.

"Marvelous," Griggs beamed. He turned to Consuela. "They gave us water while we were asleep. We don't remember a thing about it. But it proves we have nothing to fear from them."

"Oh, yeah?"

"Of course. If they wanted to harm us, they could just as easily have given us poison."

"You're trying to say something, Griggs. Say it."

Griggs smiled sheepishly. "It's just this: what's your hurry? Your helicopter's not going anywhere. You're quite safe down here—we're living proof of that. And besides, don't you realize that this is the most fantastic experience you'll ever have? That money you've got waiting in the chopper won't be a drop in the bucket to what you'll make on the lecture circuit talking about the Formigans. But you've got to know something about them before you can talk about them."

"I see. You don't want to come."

Griggs, his senses swimming in the balmy scent, shook his head. "Not now. Not just yet. Opportunities like this come to anthropologists roughly once every thousand years. I can't let it go by."

"But a minute ago, back there, you couldn't wait to get out of here."

"Really?" His brow wrinkled with an effort to remember.

"Okay, Griggs, suit yourself." She pretended to study her fingernails. "I guess with all that lecture money pouring in, you won't be needing the share of the payroll I promised you."

"No, no—it's all yours."

She looked at him shyly. "How long do you think you'll need down here?"

"Two or three days, maybe. If I miss anything, I can always come back. Why?"

"Just wondering how long I'd have to wait."

"Oh."

Griggs wondered too. Not how long, but whether she'd be there when he arrived. But hell, it didn't really matter. Even if she took the Rover and disappeared into the sunset, he was way ahead of the game. What he would learn here in the next few days would be sufficient to write and lecture about for the rest of his life. Furthermore, everything would be so vivid, being far beyond the range of his experience, that he was not likely to forget a single detail. There wasn't an anthropologist alive who wouldn't push a peanut from Plains to Kinshasa with his nose to be in his place right now. No—she was welcome to the Rover, the cold beer, the girlie magazines, the money in the helicopter, and whatever else struck her fancy.

He told her so as he gathered her in his arms and kissed her. "Five days—a week at the most," he promised.

"Sure, Griggs," she whispered. "I'll be watching for the lecture posters."

He patted her on her ample behind and watched as she strode down the passageway, following two guards who danced ahead.

Of her descent into the grotto of the Formigans, Consuela subconsciously remembered a journey that lasted a very long time. She was surprised to find that the way back seemed short. The three-man parade went back to the chamber where she had been "sterilized," and beyond into another passageway which led gently upward. Every hundred meters or so it would turn sharply and double back on itself. Sometimes the passageway sloped downward and sometimes it was perfectly level, but the trend was upward, of that she was sure. From time to time they passed through other chambers with corridors branching off from them, but never did they see an individual Formigan. Pink strips of fungus on either side of the passageway wall provided a dim but constant illumination, to which her eyes had gradually become accustomed, but other than the two figures doing the conga ahead of her, there was nothing to distract Consuela's attention from wary watchfulness.

For, though unafraid, she was suspicious. Questions lay dormant in the back of her mind, not so perplexing that they demanded immediate answers, but still persistent enough to remind her that she was not yet in the sunlight, and in the clear. The reasons Griggs had given her for their being brought down into the grotto were rational and convincing, but woman's instinct told her they were not the whole story. Nevertheless, she didn't care if she ever knew the whole story. She was not a scientist, nor was hers the contemplative soul which relishes life's small, hard-won discoveries. Hers was the brash spirit which grabs things and sensations on the run, and to hell with the dust stirred up in passing.

After they had been walking for half an hour or so, one of the two-man conga line stopped abruptly, arched his spindly torso almost double, and picked up an object from the floor of the passageway. It was too small for Consuela to identify. He held it to his eye for a moment, then tossed it to his brother, who gave it his goggly attention for an instant before throwing it back. The exchange developed into a game, each trying to throw it back when the other was unaware. The pebble bounced back and forth between them like a Ping-Pong ball. Consuela marveled that, despite their irregular gait, they never once dropped it.

She was becoming bored and a little tired from the uphill climb, gradual and intermittent though it was, when suddenly they arrived. A thin canopy of carelessly woven branches covered the end of the tunnel. One of the guards lifted it aside, negligently tossed the pebble out onto the jungle floor, then shuffled aside for Consuela to pass.

Straight ahead, the path led toward a patch of jungle through which the sun's rays pierced the green leaves like golden needles. There, doubtless, lay the savanna. It wasn't the route they had come, certainly, but it was a way out, and that was what mattered.

She brushed past the two guards, glowering at the silly, vacuous, grinning faces for the last time, and walked out on the jungle trail. Behind her, the canopy of branches fell. The jungle was absolutely silent. Not a leaf fluttered in the still air. Suddenly, she felt afraid.

She walked quickly down the footpath, swept clean as a hospital kitchen floor, toward the light in the distance. She kicked aside the pebble which the Formigan had discarded, and only after she had gone some way did curiosity bring her up short. She retraced her steps, bent over and picked up the stone. The light in the jungle was too feeble to tell what it was, but a few minutes later, when she stepped out upon the veld, and shaded her eyes until they became used to the incandescent brilliance of the midday sun, she had another look.

It was a stone. She had seen stones like it in the office of the Cuban shadow governor of northwest Angola. Smaller, duller, but the same kind of stone, without question.

This one was the size of her thumbnail. It was white, pear-shaped, and limpid as a dewdrop. From its depth, the sun's fires blazed back at her with all the colors of the rainbow.

It was a diamond. A pure white diamond. Biggest damned diamond she ever did see.

8

Griggs waited until Consuela and the guards had disappeared into the tunnel leading off the royal chamber, counted fifty, and glanced at Queen JEH.

I'll be back.

Without waiting for a reply, he walked swiftly through the mass of grinning Formigans to the entrance and down the tunnel. Behind him he heard the minstrels braying something by Shostakovich—it sounded like his Seventh Symphony, an excessively lugubrious work—and was glad he had chosen that moment to leave.

He lagged well behind, yet close enough to keep Consuela and her two escorts in view. Griggs would wait until they disappeared around a bend in the tunnel, and then sprint ahead, edge around the bend in his turn, and observe them until they reached the next switchback. Though subsidiary passages led off the main tunnel and the occasional chamber at irregular intervals, the byways invariably intersected the main tunnel at approximately a ninety-degree angle, while the main tunnel always turned back on itself at an angle nearer 180 degrees. That made his route easy to remember. Griggs noted, too, that despite the downward slope of a few portions of the tunnel, and some stretches of tunnel that seemed flat, the overall inclination was upward.

These observations were of small concern to Griggs. He was following mainly to ensure that no harm befell Consuela, and entirely incidentally to scout out the route in the event he changed his mind and decided to leave before he finished his quick survey of the grotto of the Formigans. Away from the royal chamber, he was annoyed to find his resolution again wavering. Was it the powerful challenge of the unknown that Queen JEH represented, which excited the spirit of scientific inquiry and stiffened his determination to remain in the grotto until he wrested away its secrets? Or was it something undefined and perhaps undefinable which made him want to linger so long as he was in the queen's presence yet vanished when he was beyond the range of those deep, penetrating eyes and allowed to intrude doubts as to the wisdom of remaining alone and weaponless in a world unknown to his own? He was sufficiently self-analytical to realize that the alluring fragrance Queen JEH emitted went far to dispel the shock of disgust that her body provoked. But he suspected that his mental flip-flops were more than simple male indecision.

At this moment, for instance, after he had been trailing Consuela and her guides for nearly half an hour, he was having second thoughts. Would not, perhaps, the best course be to leave now, and come back another day at the head of a team of well-armed scientists? Probably, but that would mean sharing the laurels and lucre he could expect for having completed the study, however cursorily, by himself.

He was still debating the alternatives when he saw a brighter light at the end of the tunnel, and faded back into the shadows as Consuela, with one last backward glance, stepped through the tunnel opening into the soft green jungle. He hurried forward to see whether she would meet the fate they had suffered earlier, when the maze of trails always ended up nowhere.

But when he got to the entrance, with the two guards already returning, passing him without so much as the light of recognition in their silly, bulging eyes, he saw her retreating back near the edge of the veld. When she passed beyond his range of vision, he hastened ahead until he reached the spot where she had disappeared.

By now she was walking toward the Range Rover, several hundred meters away. He waited until she had climbed in and started the engine before he breathed quite freely again. He wondered, as she sped back toward the camp in a cloud of dust, whether his anxiety had been exclusively on Consuela's account. For now that she was in the clear, she would be his link with the world and rescue if he didn't show up back in camp in a reasonable length of time. Then he reminded himself that he had no reason to expect that she would wait for him. He had no claim on her loyalty. Besides, she had made plain her intention to dig down to the helicopter and retrieve her stolen payroll. If, after recovering it, she remained so long as the blink of an eye for Griggs' sake—knowing that the Cuban army was hot on her trail—he would be very pleasantly surprised and have to revise all his convictions about the imperfectibility of human nature.

Griggs stepped back through the dense curtain of vegetation and walked slowly back down the forest trail. The sun was now at its zenith, and he should have been exhausted from the mental and physical exertions he had endured. Yet he felt as fresh as if he had just arisen from a full night's sleep. He wondered if it was the grotto's perfect microclimate, so unobtrusive that never once had he felt either cool or warm, or noticed the humidity, or detected a draft. How the Formigans maintained that atmospheric stability would be one of the first mysteries he would set himself to unravel. He vaguely recalled that for about each hundred meters of depth, earth temperatures rise around one degree Fahrenheit, which explains the sweltering conditions in which South African gold miners labor, sometimes working two or three miles underground. But there was no such temperature gradient apparent here: the temperature was the same near the surface as it was in Queen JEH's chamber far below.

Griggs set out for that place at a steady pace. On the way down, as on the way up, he counted the turns in the tunnel, thankful that the route was a simple flattened helix. It was quite regular, with none of the twists that he had feared would make the route impossible to commit to memory. Each turn descending was a left turn, just as each turn ascending had been a right turn. Counting from the Queen's chamber there had been exactly 116 turns. Each straight section of the tunnel averaged roughly sixty meters; the gradient he estimated at about three percent. That meant that the vertical component of each stretch averaged about two meters which, times 116, came to 232 meters—about the height of the Washington Monument—for the depth of Queen JEH's chamber. How on earth did the Formigans manage to keep it supplied with fresh air?

He'd ask her about that.

But that wasn't the first question that he asked when he returned to greet her thirty minutes later. On the way to the surface, he had become aware of a gnawing hunger that intensified with each step. He was not only famished, but thirsty. A few *indki* would satisfy his thirst, but his hunger was mainly for data to record in the book that would be the scientific sensation of the age.

Queen JEH had not moved. Indeed, he had not observed the slightest movement or change of expression since he first saw her. Her eyes seemed to be the only thing alive about her, but even her eyes exhibited only the narrowest range of inflection. They followed his as though led on a leash, but they never blinked, or twinkled with humor, or crackled with emotion. They were the cold deadly eyes of a basilisk.

The menace of her eyes made a bizarre contrast to the music that filled the air, a nasal rendition of *Home on the Range*, complete with static, perhaps taken from the little black box which had been in the possession of the Belgian missionary when the Formigans took possession of *him*. The minstrels, mechanical as ever, were performing the music with all the spirit of workers tightening bolts on a Ford assembly line. Like Queen JEH, they had apparently not moved anything except their mouths since Griggs first set eyes upon them. For all he knew, they were incapable of locomotion. Certainly their legs seemed about as motile as those of a grand piano. Except for the music, nothing had changed in the royal chamber since he had left an hour or two before—not the gaggle of guards hanging around the entrance looking stupid, not the subtly heady perfume that pervaded the chamber, not the feeling of confidence and control which the fragrance infused in him.

I'm back.

I knew you would be.

Did you know I'd be hungry, too?

Of course.

As if on cue, in trooped a caste of Formigan Griggs had not yet seen. They were *courtiers*—short, frail and insignificant. Their heads were miniature versions of the guards'—hairless, thin-nosed, with graceful rose-petal ears, and the same infuriating Smiley-button mouths. The head was set upon a shrunken torso, which appeared to be merely a base to which were attached long arms and short legs, both as flexible and featureless as lengths of rubber hose. The courtiers' one remarkable characteristic was their hands, with palms like Ping-Pong paddles and five independently opposable digits, all of equal length.

Griggs had supposed that the members of each caste were identical, as orientals appear to foreigners at first sight. But the more he observed them, the more he became aware of their individuality. The two guards who had conducted Consuela to the surface, for example—he was sure he could pick them out of the crowd: one had a slight bend in a nose unusually long, while the right ear of the other was twisted and deformed. Familiarity would doubtless reveal other differences among individuals. For all he knew, they might even have distinctive personalities, although he had yet to see any evidence of it.

The *courtiers*, as if they knew exactly what was expected of them, formed a line facing Griggs. Like a team of chefs at inspection in a Parisian restaurant, they extended their spatulate hands. In each, Queen JEH explained, was a different kind of Formigan food. He could eat as much or as little of each as he liked.

Griggs inspected the first offering. It was a familiar looking gray mushroom. He ate it. It offered no surprises. It tasted like what it was: raw mushroom.

The next course was unfamiliar, a reddish, leaflike fungus, which had the appearance of very thick pages of a book which, soaked in water, had then been dried in the sun. Griggs tried a page, and found it tough but delicious—something like the meat of ripe avocado.

The next courtier held a dozen large *indki*, two of which Griggs chewed, and found flavorful and refreshing. He then sampled in order the rest of the fungi, marveling at the diversity of taste and texture. Remarkably, when he finished, his hunger entirely satisfied, he didn't feel bloated. He decided that if he could sneak away samples of what he had just eaten, he'd put every Chinese restaurant on the West Coast out of business.

He crushed an *indki* between his palms, washed his hands briskly with the cool fluid, and wiped them on his trousers.

Great, he pronounced. Now, then—

Now you play for me.

Griggs smiled amiably. I'd like nothing more. Unfortunately, I busted the oboe. Broke it clean in two. All that's left are a handful of splinters.

A guard separated himself from the mob at the entrance of the royal chamber and bobbed up to Griggs. In his hand was an oboe. An oboe whole and without blemish. Griggs' own.

He took it wonderingly from the hands of the Formigan, who grinned. The oboe, in the dim light, showed only a faint hairline where the breaks had occurred, as though a streak of weak bleach had been applied to the finish. The join was not detectable to his touch.

How did you manage that?

My son, the healer, cured it.

There were species of fungus specifically for the repair of most types of organic tissue, he learned. The wood of the oboe, being dead, did not knit so successfully as Formigan flesh, which regenerated through the application of the appropriate fungus. Bone regeneration was similarly complete, although the rate of growth was substantially slower.

Griggs tried to conceal his excitement at this revelation by pretending to examine the oboe while Queen JEH told him of the curative powers of Formigan fungi. My God! he thought, as he turned over the possibilities in his mind, those medicinal fungi would revolutionize the practice of medicine. He'd put the croakers out of business. He wouldn't be able to lug away the Nobel Prizes they'd load him down with. Hell, he'd probably be awarded a knighthood by a grateful Queen Elizabeth. Sir Maynard Griggs, Bart. That sounded nice. How about Earl Griggs—Lord Griggs of Spanish Harlem? That sounded even better.

Play.

Griggs grinned as fatuously as any Formigan, stuck the dry reed in his mouth, and played. He played with his heart and soul and an imagination burning with his impending celebrity. He played every oboe solo he had ever learned, and when he had run out of solos, he played the themes of string quartets, concerti, symphonies, and sonatas. He played tangos, blues, jazz, bebop, rock, and of course congas, since he was, after all, in the Congo, where the name and dance originated. He improvised variations on nursery tunes, folk songs and military marches. He played for hours, pausing only to drink crushed *indki* which the *indki* courtier provided in a variety of refreshing flavors. And when he finished, drained of every last bit of music he could play on the oboe, he sat down upon the bare earth, soaked to the skin with exertion. What he needed right now, he decided, was a large handful of ice-cold, scotch-flavored *indki*—86 proof.

He relayed the wish to Queen JEH.

Have you anything more to play?

He laughed. Not a single damned tune.

You are certain?

For sure. I'm dry.

Queen JEH's eyes winked out. It was as if a switch had been thrown, and the deep menacing light behind

her eyes extinguished. Where those eyes had been cold
and deadly, they were now cold and dead. Griggs felt
the tie of empathy severed. He knew, without knowing
quite why, that nothing he thought, nothing he said
aloud, would now register with Queen JEH. The conviction was reinforced by the simultaneous disappearance of the scent that had gently but constantly wafted
his way ever since he had first recovered consciousness
in the room. He was surrounded by Formigans, as before, but he was alone. For them, he had ceased to exist.

9

The shock was only temporary. Hell, he reasoned,
after enduring them all day without interruption, anyone would have had a belly full of him and the ill
woodwind that nobody blows good. Queen JEH had
made abundantly clear her biological need for new
music to stimulate her reproductive powers. For all he
knew, her mind was incapable of communicating once
the generative cycle had begun. Indeed, he suspected
that already the first stages may have been in process,
for the minstrels were in full voice, repeating the music
he had just played, deafeningly but with perfect fidelity, including flatted notes. And the guards and courtiers had disappeared.

Griggs decided that perhaps being ignored was to his
advantage. The minstrels would be busy reproducing
his music the rest of the day—or was it night? Meanwhile, he would be inspecting the Formigan realm.
There would be questions unanswered. He would see if

Queen JEH was more receptive to them after her minstrels had done their work.

He started, methodically, at the first branch leading off from the helical ramp to the surface. Fearful he might become lost if he weren't careful, he made rigorous mental notes of his route—the distance, the turns, the gradients—so that he would have no trouble retracing his steps.

For the first ten minutes he plodded steadily forward through empty corridors and chambers, not once encountering a Formigan. This was odd if, as Queen JEH asserted—and he had no reason to disbelieve—there were legions of Formigans inhabiting this nether world. He dismissed his doubts with the thought that the tunnels must extend mile upon mile. Indeed, this was most likely if the Formigans had lived here for three thousand years and more. He decided that these must be living areas long abandoned.

The illumination in the passageway he was traversing was dimmer than in the main tunnel from which he had branched off. Did this mean that the supply of the fungus was restricted, or was another factor operative? He thought he found the answer when he came to another half dozen passages leading off the main tunnel and entered the first of them.

It was so dark he could barely see. He felt his way along until he could no longer discern light from the direction in which he had come. In the darkness and silence, he lost all sensation of the passage of time. But fatigue told him that he had gone far enough. He sat down on the ground and leaned against the wall, resting while he thought over what he had seen—or rather, had not seen.

He had been walking at a fair pace for a long time—how long, he could not guess, for it had been many months since he had stopped wearing a watch. In Africa, one didn't need a watch: sunrise, high noon, and sunset were enough. But here, where there was no sun, he wished he could tell how much time had gone by, for it would have given him a measure of the ground he had covered.

So far, he hadn't encountered a single Formigan. He hadn't seen a single artifact, or fungus garden, or depot of leaves and jungle-floor debris on which a fungus garden could be raised. He hadn't seen anything at all. There were two obvious explanations: the first, based on the information given by Queen JEH, was that, if thousands of Formigans indeed inhabited these tunnels, they all must be concentrated in some other part of the Formigan Kingdom. Alternatively, if the population was dispersed, these tunnels must run for thousands of kilometers underground for him not to have seen any Formigans. The law of averages forbade any other interpretation. The alternative conclusion was that the vast Formigan population existed only in Queen JEH's imagination—or perhaps her belly. Griggs himself had seen only a couple of hundred, altogether, counting the *guards, courtiers,* and *minstrels.* But if she had deceived him, why had she done so?

It certainly wasn't to intimidate him with their numbers, in order to keep him too frightened to try to escape. After all, he was quite willing to stay without coercion. Furthermore, the Queen had willingly allowed Consuela to leave. And he had followed Consuela to make sure she was not detained outside his ken. It was a puzzle. And while he pondered it, fatigue finally overcame him. His eyes grew heavy, the blackness around him closed in upon his senses, and he fell asleep.

When he awoke, refreshed but with aching muscles, the tunnel where he lay had become appreciably brighter.

The lighting wasn't uniform. The extremities of the tunnel, indeed, were still obscure. But closer to him, the strips of fungi on both sides of the passageway glowed. And the nearer the fungi were, the brighter the glow. Experimentally, he put his hand against the strip of illuminating fungus. Nothing happened; it wasn't body heat that stimulated the fungus to fluorescence. The movement of air caused by his passage through the tunnel might conceivably have been the cause. He tested this hypothesis by fanning the strip with his hand. No change.

That reduced the options considerably. One of few remaining he examined by putting his face close to the strip and exhaling. He was rewarded by a tiny but immediate brightening of a rectangle half a meter long, diminishing in intensity toward the extremities. He slapped his hands together in smug satisfaction. He had reduced the reasonable explanations to two: either it was the moisture in his breath that caused the fluorescence, or it was the carbon dioxide. There was no easy way to test which of the two assumptions was correct, but to make sure that what he had done was no fluke, he walked a dozen paces down the tunnel and again breathed softly on the illuminating strip. It produced enough light to read by.

It produced something else—a distinct chill in the air, and the heady sensation of a whiff of pure oxygen. If it *was* oxygen, then the fungus must be metabolizing the carbon dioxide he exhaled, converting the carbon fraction into luminescence and releasing oxygen as a by-product. Griggs' recollection of the chemistry lab was pretty shaky, but it seemed a reasonable surmise.

That premise also led to several conclusions. First, the passageways he had been traversing were used by the oxygen-breathing Formigans, even if he hadn't seen any: otherwise there would have been no source of carbon dioxide for the fungi to metabolize. Second, the fungi's utilization of carbon dioxide for luminescence was very efficient, for the spots on which he had breathed directly were still bright, and showed no signs of dimming. Nor was a mechanical means of ventilation necessary in the Formigan realm, whose oxygen–carbon dioxide balance was self-regulating: when the Formigans breathed, both light and oxygen were produced by the CO_2-absorbing fungi. As for the chilled air, he attributed that to the endothermic nature of the chemical reaction: the fungus needed thermal energy to power the reaction, and in extracting it from the ambient air, the fungus acted as a cooling system.

Griggs saw instantly that the bioluminescent fungus alone was a scientific discovery of the first magnitude.

Its applications on the surface of the Earth—providing it could be cultivated there—would be of enormous importance. Used in highrise office buildings and apartments, it would eliminate the necessity for air conditioning and ventilating systems, not to mention windows for lighting. In manned space vehicles, the fungus would reduce significantly the weight devoted to batteries and oxygen bottles, thus liberating cargo capacity for additional payload. Bacteria-free environments for hospital isolation wards could be contrived using pure strains of the fungus. The horizons were infinite.

Before he started selling the stuff by the pound, however, Griggs thought it advisable to test his theories. That took breathing bodies, and the only place he knew to find them was in Queen JEH's royal chamber.

He retraced his steps there.

Nobody noticed his arrival. The minstrels were performing "Old Man River," scored for solo oboe, and Queen JEH was apparently living in another world, for her eyes were closed. That seemed reasonable, for there was nothing to look at except the minstrels, and she had seen them before. Of the guards and courtiers, there was still no sign.

The oboe has a range from B-flat below to third G above middle C. That gave most of the heftier minstrels, whose large chests were built for resonating the bass notes, a holiday. They just stood like a clutch of naked clothes dummies, with their mouths closed. Griggs decided to put them to work.

He walked down the line to a minstrel who looked as though he might be responsible for a note in the range of about B♯ to F♭ and leaned over for a good look. This one, in common with the others, was built like a turnip set upon diminutive legs. The top of his smooth bald head just reached Griggs' second shirt button, reading from the top. His eyes were open and unblinking, and he didn't seem at all aware of Griggs' presence. His mouth was closed. He had no arms at all, not even stumps. His head was joined to his torso by a thick white neck merging into broad shoulders that narrowed to tiny rudimentary legs and even tinier feet. The total effect of the little Formigan minstrel was one of a children's top the instant it stops spinning, a fraction of a second before it topples over. Thinking of the simile, Griggs blew gently on the minstrel.

The minstrel toppled over backward, rolled erratically around on the floor of the chamber for a moment, then came to a standstill, lying on his side. Griggs leaned over and picked him up. He was astonished to find that the bass minstrel weighed in like a falsetto: he could lift two of them with ease.

He did so. He tucked one under each arm, and carried them to the entrance of the chamber and into the tunnel.

On returning, he carefully noted the level of bioluminescence in the throne room. Apparently it had not altered. But by the time he had made twenty trips transporting the whole bass section, the light was fading fast. Griggs smiled. His little experiment was a success: the pink fungus did indeed metabolize CO_2 exhaled by the Formigans. In its turn, it absorbed ambient heat and produced light and oxygen.

The quantities of CO_2 and O_2, furthermore, were in equilibrium. This meant that, had he known more chemistry than he learned from college courses taken years before, he could compute the efficiency of the light production process from the amounts of heat and carbon absorbed. He dismissed the thought: it would provide grist for a raft of Ph.D. theses in biochemistry one of these days. He could see the typical dedication now: "To that world-renowned savant, Dr. Maynard Griggs, who made this study possible, with respect and deep humility."

He interrupted his daydream to see whether Queen JEH was still lost in dreams of her own. She wasn't. The moment his eyes caught hers, he was conscious of her commanding presence.

Bring back my minstrels. At once.

Griggs smiled complacently. He wasn't afraid of this

cave full of cream puffs, and he thought it was about time to let them know it.

What's the rush, Your Majesty? Got a hot date someplace?

Now.

Griggs was conscious that the lovely fragrance did not accompany her words. He shrugged.

The next thing he remembered was that he couldn't breathe. He had inhaled liquid fire. He clutched his throat, but only because he had but two hands. The fiery agony went all the way to his toes. For what seemed forever he gasped, trying to get a breath of air, but his throat was blocked by a huge fireball. His eyes rolled back and he fell in a heap to the floor.

Then, as suddenly as the spasm of agony had come, it departed, as though it had never been. There wasn't the slightest hint of difficulty in breathing. The only evidence that he had suffered excruciating distress was a slight hint of ozone in the air, as after an electrical storm.

He looked at Queen JEH.

Now.

Anything you say, Queen.

He scrambled to his feet and set off down the tunnel. There he tucked two of the minstrels under his arms and hastened back to the royal chamber to deposit them where, to the best of his recollection, he had found them. He experienced a bit of difficulty in balancing them on their tiny feet. It was as frustrating as setting up ten pins on a fishing boat. The minstrels didn't seem to mind. As for their mates, they were wrapped up in *Deep Purple* and oblivious of all else.

Griggs had retrieved all but three or four of the minstrels, and was busy setting up the most recent arrivals when he heard a familiar voice behind him.

"What's all this, Griggs—moving day?"

10

A glow of warmth suffused Griggs' cheeks, and he was glad that on his dark skin it wouldn't show, for he was sensitive about being thought sentimental. Sentimentality was strictly a woman's trait. Still, he had to admit to himself a pleasure very much akin to tenderness in the Cuban woman's return. If ever a man was certain that a woman's actions were motivated by selfless concern for him, and nothing else, Griggs was that man. Why else would she have come back?

"What are you doing here?" he asked gruffly and, he felt, a little superfluously.

"You need looking after," she replied quietly, averting her eyes.

He laughed. "If I'd known you were coming back, I'd have given you a shopping list."

"Really? From what you told me, they have everything you need down here."

"Yes, down here. I want it up there. If you had used your head, you'd have realized that I need sterile containers to preserve samples of the fungi for analysis."

She bridled. "How on Earth do you expect me—an army paymaster—to know about things like that? . . . What kind of containers?"

He shrugged. "Oh, test tubes—there's a wire basket of them on the bookshelf, glassine envelopes, slides, cover glasses—"

She opened a brown canvas bag hanging from her shoulder and displayed its contents. "You mean these things?" she said innocently.

"Well, well," he said admiringly, "I guess the average Cuban is pretty dumb, after all."

Consuela bristled. "What do you mean by that?"

He gathered her up in his arms and planted a kiss on her cheek.

"It's obvious, Consuela. If the rest of them had a tenth of your brains, Castro wouldn't have lasted a minute."

"That's pretty zippy thinking for a damned *yanqui*," she said, not disengaging his arms. "I hope we're not shocking the natives."

"Screw the natives."

"Ugh!" she said, looking at Queen JEH over his shoulder, inadvertently establishing communications when she had her mind elsewhere.

You have returned to sing for me.

"Well—uh—I guess I have."

"You have?" Griggs said, holding her out at arm's length. "I thought you found them repulsive."

"Who? . . . Oh," she said, nodding toward Queen JEH, "Old barge-belly had my eye, Griggs. She wanted to know if I've come back to sing for her, and I told her yes, I guess I have."

He turned to Queen JEH. "Guess again, sister. I've just been appointed sole booking agent for Srta. Consuela Millán y Gorgas. She sings when I tell her to sing."

Then tell her to sing.

"I will. About ten minutes worth."

Queen JEH's eyes flamed like an erupting volcano.

"Ten minutes is about all she can sing at one time, you see. Gets all tense in the throat. Has to walk around a bit to loosen up. And since we're walking, I think we'd like to make an escorted tour of your realm. Do we understand each other? And," he said quickly, pointing his finger at her in a minatory manner, "I'd suggest you save the pharynx fireball-trick for another time: Consuela just might lose her voice altogether if she sees me suffering."

There was a slight pause as Queen JEH's malevolent eyes studied him. Then:

Sing.

Griggs nodded to Consuela.

Consuela sang.

Griggs was again astonished to hear the sweet, virginal soprano voice emanating from that lusty female body. It was as incongruous as a recitation of W. H. Auden blank verse by a Los Angeles Rams linebacker. She sang Olympia's aria from *The Tales of Hoffman,* performed as if before an audience of thousands. She finished with arms outstretched, as if expecting to be showered with bouquets and cries of "Brava!"

Griggs applauded.

"You really *are* good."

She smiled shyly.

"Coffee break, Queen JEH," said Griggs rising, briskly. "Tell one of your sons to take us around. I want to see everything."

You shall see everything.

Two Formigans of the guard caste detached themselves from the group and bobbed down the passageway, followed by Griggs and Consuela.

Griggs noted that they were the same two guards who had guided them before—the one with the long nose and the other with the cauliflower ear.

"I don't mind admitting that I'm grateful that you came back," Griggs said.

"You mean the test tubes and stuff? Oh, that's nothing."

"It's not the test tubes—not that I'm sorry to have them, of course—it's you."

"Got lonely, did you?"

"Yes, I did." He put his arm around her waist and drew her closer. She laid her head in the crook of his shoulder. However, as she was as tall as he, this bent her neck in an awkward and painful manner, and she removed it and put her arm over his shoulder instead. That was more comfortable, but killed the romantic effect. "Did you get a good night's sleep?" he asked.

"No. I had something on my mind. Couldn't stop thinking about it."

He slid his left hand up under her jacket until her

breast was cradled in his palm. "So did I," he lied,
"but it's nothing we can't take care of now that you've
come back."

Until he said that, she had been on the verge of telling him, but now she didn't have the heart. That she
had discovered diamonds in the Formigan kingdom
couldn't but be a welcome revelation, but not at the
price of destroying his male ego. The surprise would
keep.

"Sure," she said lightly. "We can sell season tick-
ets."

"And build a grandstand to accommodate the
crowd."

"Not forgetting door prizes."

"And blue-movie rights. We'll be a sensation."

"And speaking of sensations," she said, stopping in
her tracks, "I've just had one."

"Something you can share?"

"I forgot the bag with the test tubes and things. I'll
have to go back. Won't take me a minute."

"Wait, Connie, let me—" he began, but she was already moving at a brisk pace back the way they had
come, while their guides were dancing on ahead, oblivious of having lost their following. Griggs caught up
with them and laid restraining hands on their rubbery
arms. "Hold everything," he said, pointing at the retreating figure. "She's forgot her knitting."

The Formigans grinned. . . .

Consuela Millán y Gorgas marched back into the
royal chamber with a confident tread. She had not, like
Griggs, learned of the throat-searing consequences of
defying the Queen of the Formigans. She had left the
Formigan realm as effortlessly as walking out her own
front door, and she had returned to it of her own free
will. She knew that Queen JEH very much wanted—
needed, for the very survival of her species—the music
she had still to sing. She was, therefore, quite unin-
timidated by the sulfurous stare that greeted her.

"See this?" Consuela said, reaching into her voluminous patch pocket and bringing out the rough diamond. "Do you know what this is?"

It is a pebble. A pebble whose eye, like the eye of Queen JEH, never blinks. It is an evil eye.

Hey, thought Consuela, this is going to be easier than I thought.

What is going to be easier than you thought?

"I came back here to help you, didn't I?" said Consuela, recovering smoothly, and reminding herself to look away when she wanted to think private thoughts. "Well, I'm not only going to sing for you—I'm going to take away every evil eye I find. How do you like them onions?"

Onions—what are onions?

"I mean, do you dig—are you—does that please you?"

If you take them away they shall be gone. It is predestined.

"Now you're talking, Queen. Tell me, where can I find more of these evil eyes, so I can get rid of them for you?"

They peek from the walls of the grotto of the Formigans, watching what we do, spying upon us.

Consuela walked over to the nearest wall, threading her way between the minstrels who were, she suddenly realized, performing Olympia's aria in exact but earsplitting imitation of her own voice. She ran her fingers along the smooth dark surface of the wall, feeling for protuberances. There were none. But the wall itself was suggestive—hard, slate-gray to black in color, and with the texture of glass. She had overheard enough camp gossip and get-rich-quick banter during her months in Angola to realize that this was the "blue ground" they were always dreaming about—kimberlite, the core of some primeval volcano which, under immense pressure, had crystalized chunks of pure carbon into clear, sparkling gems.

The grotto of the Formigans was one vast diamond mine.

11

Griggs was beginning to wonder what had happened to Consuela when he saw her in the distance, rounding a bend in the tunnel. She walked with the chin-high, straight-shouldered swagger of the professional soldier, from the waist up. Down below it was a different story. Her pelvis seemed to have a life of its own. It undulated in about four planes simultaneously, proceeding on a corkscrew course that led unerringly to his own, as she came up to him with a gentle bump, and kissed him on the nose.

"Miss me?" she asked.

"Can't—ain't built that way," he replied gravely, "but I'd be happy to mister you."

"Tonight," she promised. "But right now, I think we'd better save our strength for whatever our googleeyed little friends have to show us. Lead on, little ones," she said to the Formigans, who had been preening themselves and each other with their rubbery appendages in what Griggs, who had turned away after one shocked look, thought an unnecessarily obscene manner.

They seemed to understand, for they immediately stopped what they were doing and resumed their shuffle down the dim pink corridor. Soon the tunnel widened into a cavern as large as a railway station. From it issued no less than forty branches. Unhesitatingly, the Formigans plunged into the first of them. No doubt about it—these were the fungus farms of which Queen JEH had told Griggs.

The first wasn't much to see. It was simply a chamber, about two hundred meters long, with a ceiling so low that the guides' heads barely cleared it. Down the center ran a narrow walkway on either side of which were beds of fungi stretching the length of the chamber. The fungus here was of the consistency of steel wool, matted and springy. When Griggs broke off a sample to put in a test tube, it made his fingers tingle as though immersed in weak acid.

It didn't seem to bother the planters, though. There were two of them, one on each side. Their legs, rubbery and boneless like those of the guides, terminated in forked, spadelike appendages they used to work the humus on which the fungus grew, like Italian peasants treading grapes. Their jointless arms were so long that they could tend the fungus without bending over, plucking a strand of fungus from one clump of growth to thin it out, then staggering on their cloven hoofs like drunken ballet dancers to transplant the growth on a bare spot some distance away, their faces wreathed in perpetual grins. They ignored their visitors completely, and went about their work with such absorption that Griggs wondered whether they were equipped with the senses necessary to apprehend the presence of interlopers such as they.

From each of the tunnels they visited, Griggs abstracted a sample of the fungus which grew there, put it in a test tube, stoppered and labeled it with a grease pencil, and added it to the growing collection in Consuela's canvas bag. He recognized a few of the fungi as those he had eaten, but the function of the others remained a mystery. That they had some vital use in the community was proven by their cultivation; it would take a more rigorous study than he could devote to the subject now, however, to determine just what that function might be. He was gratified to note that every fifth or sixth tunnel contained *indki*, which seemed to confirm his guess that this fungus had an indispensible role in maintaining the water balance in the grotto of the Formigans.

Afterward he could never guess how many hours

they spent in that tour of exploration. They walked until their legs ached, but always around the next tunnel bend the unknown drew them on. They saw fungi in dozens of colors, in dozens of shapes and configurations, some tiny, some gigantic—such as the huge round puffballs so filling one nursery that they occasionally had to crawl on their hands and knees to get by. Some were pleasantly odoriferous, some stinking, some velvety to the touch, others as rough as sandpaper. But all were lovely to the eye of the scientist.

Before Griggs and Consuela became so tired they could scarcely plod forward another step, they had looked at, touched, smelled or tasted more than two hundred individual species of fungus, mold, yeast, or slime. They let their Formigan guides, whom they had dubbed Pat and Mike, be their canon as to their handling of the fungi. If Pat and Mike ate of the fungus, so did they. If Pat and Mike demonstrated how *emusdor* worked by grabbing up a handful, rubbing it against a wall, and half a minute later tapping it with a soft finger and stepping back while half a ton of friable earth slumped to the tunnel floor, they did the same. Upon leaving each tunnel, like Pat and Mike they submitted to the ritual cleansing of their spore-impregnated bodies by the feathery-limbed healers stationed at the entrances, who whisk-broomed them thoroughly before the party proceeded to the next species of fungus, slime, or mold.

It was fascinating, but very exhausting. Finally, although Pat and Mike seemed as fresh as ever, Griggs and Consuela tried to make them understand by gesture that they had to rest. Pat and Mike grinned, and went waltzing ahead.

"I can't, Griggs," Consuela moaned.

"One more won't kill you," he replied, the scientist getting the better of the man.

"All right," she said resignedly. "Just one."

She let Griggs take the lead, and kept alert for the telltale glint that had so far betrayed the presence of three diamonds, any one of which would make them rich when they got out of this eerie place. She smiled, thinking how surprised and pleased Griggs would be, and how she would twit him for having his head in the scientific clouds, too preoccupied to look down, where a single colored stone which glinted up at him would be worth all the lectures he could deliver in a lifetime.

She fondled the diamonds in her pocket—a yellow and two blue-whites. The smallest would cover an American penny and the largest, an oblong stone, was the size of the third joint of her little finger. She was far from expert, but she had seen enough diamonds to know that these three alone should be worth as much as a million dollars; if flawless, much more. The contemplation of such a huge sum so absorbed her thoughts that, for a moment, she paid no attention when her ankle almost turned on a pebble lying in her path. When she realized what it might be, she retraced her steps and dropped to one knee.

"What's the matter?" called Griggs.

"Nothing—nothing at all," said Consuela. "Just tying my shoelace."

But when she rose, the three diamonds had become four.

The last chamber, which seemed to roll out for hundreds of meters into the distance, was drenched in the musty, rotting smell of the forest floor. This, as Griggs soon perceived, was because the tunnel was blanketed with arboreal refuse—leaves, twigs, vines, bark, decaying logs and grasses, dead rodents and small reptiles. Among them, in a profusion so dense that they had to force their way through it as though walking waist-deep in water, grew a species of fungus which was new to Griggs' experience. It ranged from light gray when small and undeveloped to shiny black when fully grown, when it reached the roof of the tunnel high overhead. It was a smooth, stalklike fungus with rounded protuberances along its entire length, like bulging eyes puffed with sleep. The stalks waved gently to and fro, and Griggs was reminded of seaweed undulating in the ocean depths, until he realized that since there was not the slightest breath of a breeze, the fungus was moving by itself. Griggs suddenly wished he was someplace else, and was willing to suspend the imperative of scientific enquiry to be there. A glance at Consuela told him he was not alone.

But the Formigans plunged right into the billowing mass of fungi and left Griggs and Consuela no option but to follow. They had waded through more of the fungus than they cared to think about—for, in addition to its sinister movement the stalks felt slimy to the touch—when the color of the stalks began to change. Griggs couldn't decide whether it was the presence of humans, or of Formigans, or whether it was something entirely unrelated, as for example a phase in their growth. Whatever the cause, the black adult fungus began to lighten. Pat and Mike stopped, and remained motionless. Griggs and Consuela followed their example.

As they watched, the black luster of the slimy adult fungus—it was only the adult that changed hue—shaded into a deep purple, then slowly to magenta, to scarlet, to cherry, and then to a flame red. As the red reached its peak of brightness, the Formigans suddenly grabbed the base of a stalk in each hand and snapped them off as effortlessly as if they were rotten string. At once the chromatic process of the forest of fungi shifted into reverse—to cherry and through scarlet and magenta back to pitch black. Until the fungus reached its original hue, the Formigans stood still, then beat a rapid retreat the way they had come, dragging their stalks, which alone remained flame red, behind them.

Because they were bulkier, Griggs and Consuela followed at a slower pace, until they realized that the slimy tendrils, which had heretofore swayed in random fashion, were now bending toward them, wrapping themselves around their arms and legs. In panic, Griggs plunged forward toward the disappearing Formigans, who slithered nimbly and unconcernedly out of the fungi's wet embrace.

As he bent forward, tearing loose slimy, octopuslike tendrils from his legs, they wrapped themselves around his torso, his neck, and finally his face. A thin fluid oozed from the protuberances of the black tendrils, flowed in a rivulet down his cheek, and into his mouth, gaping from the exertion of clearing a path. He spat out the liquid as if it was poison, aware that it well might be. But no sooner was one thick black arm disengaged than another took its place. Yet, the embrace, though disgusting, was never overpowering—a glance back at Consuela told him that she was clawing away the tendrils with as little difficulty as he—and he couldn't explain, even to himself, why he was consumed with unreasoning fear.

Soon his face was bathed in the exudate of the fungus, and spitting became a reflex, as it did with Consuela laboring behind him in his tracks. No longer was it a question of simply breaking away from any individual strand of the fungus, for that he could do without difficulty, but of having the strength and stamina to keep going until they got clear of the morass of undulating, slimy black horrors.

It was by accident that he found the solution. Until then, he had been yanking away each enveloping tendril as it fastened upon him. But when exhaustion finally tripped him up, and he tumbled in a heap among the roots of the accursed plant, in desperation he grabbed it at the base, where it was thickest, twisting it in sudden rage as if it were the neck of a human enemy. It snapped off like a rotten twig. The tentacles clutching his windpipe relaxed and fell away instantly, and he found himself free.

Of course! What he did was exactly what the Formigans themselves had done, and he cursed himself for not having realized that the Formigans, in their weakness, could subdue the tenacious black fungus only by attacking it at a vulnerable point.

It made sense, too. It takes a pair of six-ton trucks to pull a piece of bamboo apart, yet it can be broken in two with relative ease. It was clear to Griggs that the stealthy menace of the prehensile plant had clouded his mind, making him forget his junglecraft and common sense alike. He thanked god they had returned in time.

He began snapping off the offending plant at the roots and flinging the pieces out of their path in a frenzy of destruction that left him panting from the exertion but exhilarated in conquering an enemy that almost had him beaten. He charged through the black forest of fungus, ripping it apart with a savage glee, until at last, just ahead, he perceived Pat and Mike at the tunnel entrance, together with its attendant *healer*. Pulling Consuela along behind him, he stumbled clear of the last strands of fungus seeking to embrace them, and sank to the floor. Griggs wiped his face on his sleeve, and then applied his shirt tail to Consuela's, gently dabbing away the sweat mixed with the alien fungal fluid, dust, and bits of grass and bark that had adhered to her face during their flight from the black horror. Too weak to speak, she thanked him with haggard eyes, which then closed in a flutter of long lashes as she sank into a deep, dreamless sleep.

Griggs lifted her head and rested it on his shoulder. Then, with a sigh, he too gave himself up to overpowering fatigue. Just as he was dropping off, he glanced up at Pat and Mike, hovering by his side, grinning. He raised his middle finger in an obscene salute and muttered "Up yours," and fell sound asleep.

A healer came forward with outspread winglike appendages to perform his familiar cleansing ritual. Like a conductor leading his orchestra in a *largo* movement, his wings dipped and floated over the recumbent figures of Griggs and Consuela. From the edges of the transparent membrane that connected his long fingers drifted a silvery powder, covering the sleepers in a gossamer layer of dust. The healer stepped back. In a few moments, the film of dust seemed to fluoresce faintly, then disappeared. The healer turned and went back to the entrance of the cavern of the black fungus, again to take up his lonely vigil.

By and by, Pat and Mike were joined by two other Formigans. They were of a caste which Queen JEH had neglected to mention to Griggs: the *inseminators*. They were virtually the same as the healers in every feature save the arms. Instead of feathery, winglike appendages, the inseminators had no arms at all.

One of the inseminators knelt before Griggs. Putting

his small round head close to the black man's skin, he
slowly passed his lips over Griggs' entire body, depositing a greenish dew. He rose and gave way to the other
inseminator, who performed the same rite on Consuela,
except that the dew was a royal red.

The inseminators returned, silently, the way they
came.

Consuela and Griggs never stirred, and before the
inseminators had disappeared down the tunnel, the dew
they left behind had vanished, too.

12

Griggs sat up and rubbed the sleep out of his eyes.
He had no idea how long he had been sleeping, but it
was long enough to invigorate him completely. Some
hours, at least, he decided, for the tunnel fungi glowed
brightly from prolonged exposure to the carbon dioxide
of their exhalations. He stood up and stretched, and
felt that he was ready for anything the Formigans had
to offer. He was certainly ready for Consuela Millán y
Gorgas, who at that moment appeared around a bend
in the tunnel, buttoning her baggy green trousers.

"Watering the plants," she explained.

"So I see. How do you feel?"

"Terrific. I'm so hungry I could eat a horse."

Griggs neighed.

She regarded him smokily. "I'm a girl who doesn't
take nay for an answer," she whispered, snuggling up
to him.

With his free hand Griggs unbuttoned her battle

jacket, a garment well-named, for it was there, and then, that battle was joined. . . .

Griggs rested his head on her bare midriff, and wished dreamily that he was a smoker. Clearly, this was a moment when a cigarette would have been rewarding. But her hand stroking his brow was certainly just as satisfying, and perhaps even more habit forming. It was something he would have to think about—whether this was a habit he wanted to get into, having got into practically everything else where Consuela was concerned.

"Say—" she began.

"Anything you want," he replied. "Especially yes."

"I know that. No, I was wondering—where are Pat and Mike?"

"Who cares?"

"Well, we don't have them to guide us, how will we keep from getting lost?"

"Not to worry," Griggs reassured her. "This is the fungi farm belt isn't it?"

"Yes."

"And the Formigans eat, don't they?"

"Yes."

"Well, then—if they want to eat, they have to pass this way, and when they do, we'll be right here where they can't miss us."

Consuela was pensive. "Yes, I've been thinking about that, Griggs. We've seen enough food in the past few hours to feed a regiment—an army. But where's the army?"

"Oh, around," Griggs replied airily. "After all, there are miles of tunnels. Maybe *hundreds* of miles of tunnels. Remember, this kingdom has been in existence at least since the time of Hanno."

"Han who?"

"Hanno, the Carthaginian. He's the bloke who, according to Herodotus, set sail from Carthage about 500 B.C. going west toward the Pillars of Hercules—the Straits of Gibraltar, to you—and turned up three years later, coming from the *east*. He told his countrymen that he sailed for the first half of his voyage with the rising sun on his left hand, while during the second half the sun rose on his right hand."

"Very handy—but I don't get the point."

"Simple. He sailed through the Straits of Gibraltar into the Atlantic, turned southward along the coast of Africa, and sailed all the way down to the Cape of Good Hope, with the rising sun, you will note, on his left. Coming back up along the coast on the Indian Ocean side of Africa, the rising sun was on his right. In short, he circumnavigated Africa a thousand years before the Portuguese, but of course it was all wasted effort. The Carthaginians didn't know that Africa was a continent, and they probably stoned him to death for telling them such an outrageous sea story. But the point is, on his outward leg, two of his sailors jumped ship, and wound up as guests of one of her Majesty Queen JEH's predecessors. That's where the Formigans heard of the 'strange abode which fled from the winds across the waters'—obviously Hanno's ship. Just think—two deserters from the Punic merchant marine have wandered down these very corridors."

"Think that's them?" asked Consuela, pointing.

In the distance, two figures came bobbing toward them. It could have been the roll of the ship that the Carthaginian sailors hadn't worked out of their sea legs, but Griggs was inclined to believe that the figures approaching were those of their dear old friends, Pat and Mike.

And indeed, the grinning Formigans who danced up to them a few moments later were Pat and Mike. Griggs addressed them: "Look, boys, don't think we're not grateful for the grand tour of your plantations, but we'd like to get on, see something else. How about it?"

The Formigans grinned. From somewhere behind their Smiley-button mouths came a faint buzz, like an electric razor behind a bathroom's closed door. Griggs had heard it before, and wondered whether it might be a feature of the Formigans' extrasensory communications apparatus.

"Like the *memorialists*, for instance. I'd sure like—"

But the Formigans had already set off, perhaps in

response to some telepathic command of Queen JEH. As they waddled down the passageway, Griggs and Consuela looked at each other, shrugged, and followed in their wake.

"What do you think they did with those repulsive red *things* they dragged out of that horrible cavern?" asked Consuela, shuddering at the recollection of the slimy tentacles embracing her.

"Beats me." But Griggs was glad the duo had gotten rid of them, whatever they were. What the function of the oily red stalks was Griggs could not imagine. He made a mental note to ask Queen JEH the next time around.

Up ahead, Pat and Mike had disappeared. One moment they were out in front, bouncing along around a bend in the passageway, the next they had just vanished in thin air. Griggs and Consuela advanced until they were at about the point where Pat and Mike had last been seen. They looked about them. In the dim light, at first they could detect no clue to the missing Formigans. Then Griggs spotted a faint blotch on the wall just ahead of him. He took two quick steps forward and looked again. In that brief moment, the blotch had shrunk to the size of his palm, and while he stared at it, comprehension slowly dawning, it disappeared entirely.

"Come here, Connie."

She came to his side. "What's up?"

"They're here." He pointed at the wall. "They've got to be. There's no place else they could have gone."

"I don't see anything but wall."

"That's reasonable, because that's what you're looking at."

"Then—"

"They're behind it. Unlimber that bag of yours."

She took the canvas bag from her shoulder and set it gingerly on the ground. Griggs unfastened the flap and went through its contents, test tube by test tube. There were some forty of them, and half of them held specimens. Another four score specimens of fungus and slime were contained in sealed glassine envelopes. In collecting the samples, Griggs had worked by a rule-of-thumb according to which those fungi, slimes, and molds which seemed most useful, mysterious, or bizarre, went into test tubes. For what appeared to be more run-of-the-mill myxomycetes, he employed glassine envelopes. Now he was searching for his test tube of *emusdor*, the hydrophilic fungus which, when applied to soil, sucked out every molecule of water, leaving behind an easily friable mass of dry earth.

It was obvious that Pat and Mike, unless they somehow had mastered the feat of vanishing into thin air, had entered a branch passageway and, once inside, perhaps as a Formiganstyle practical joke, had applied the slime mold *rodsume* to the entrance. It had almost instantaneously closed the gap with its intertwining tendrils, and in another second or two would, in the faint light, have become indistinguishable from the rest of the tunnel wall. The faint difference in tone he had observed must have been the hole actually closing the entrance to a chamber slightly better illuminated than the passageway in which they now found themselves.

"This is it," he said, holding up the test tube against the luminous fungus strip so that he could read the red-wax writing on the glass. " *'Emusdor.'* Hand me one of those cotton swabs." He uncorked the test tube carefully, inserted the swab she produced into its neck, and picked up a tiny smear of fungus. Corking the tube, he handed it to her to put back with the others and vigorously applied the smear to the wall. He waited a moment, then tapped it, experimentally.

Nothing happened. This was strange. When he had been guided through the cavern where this particular fungus was cultivated, he had observed that it was growing on a bed of a cool, glasslike material, which to his amazement seemed also to be constituted of some living substance, for its transparency unaccountably waxed and waned in the dim cavern light. From the first, he had been alert to test each fungus to determine which was *rodsume* and which *emusdor*, for he considered these two fungi potentially the most useful in the world outside. He had therefore touched a clod of earth picked up from the cavern floor to the cultivated fungi. Almost at once the clod seemed to come alive. It was as if a tiny elf were inside, kicking to be let out. He dropped it as though it were a hot coal. It fell to the ground, disintegrating into a million particles of dust. He had immediately filled a test tube with the fungus and labeled it, with a certainty born of experience, *emusdor*. But something had happened to it to make it lose its efficacy, apparently, for the wall still stood, visibly unaffected.

"Well, genius?" Consuela smirked.

"That's funny," Griggs mused.

"I'm laughing."

"It's the right stuff—no doubt about it."

"Sure it is," she agreed, grinning wolfishly. "Want to try another medicine, doctor? Or maybe the old bitch has been stringing you along, and you don't want to admit it?"

He tapped the wall again. His knuckles thudded against it hollowly.

They waited. They waited for several minutes, looking at the blank wall, while their faith in *emusdor* crumbled.

"Shit!" Griggs exclaimed finally, and slammed his fist against the smooth black surface.

It collapsed into dust. A hole appeared. It wasn't anything like doorsize, but it was big enough to crawl through, and Griggs promptly did so. Consuela followed, with less success, her hips jamming tight in the aperture. Griggs grabbed her by the arms and heaved, and she popped out like a cork from a bottle.

"What the hell!" she whispered, awestruck.

13

They were in an immense high-domed chamber, whose confines appeared to stretch out to infinity. The chamber was perfectly flat, and illuminated by rings of light which lay, with absolute symmetry, on the floor as far as the eye could see. The rings, apparently of the same pink bioluminescent fungus which everywhere lit the grotto of the Formigans, were about five meters in diameter, and each separated from the next by the same interval.

In the center of each circle of light sat a figure, as squat as a fireplug, with an enormous head resting on a tiny body. The facial features were very much the same as those of Pat and Mike, and approximately of the same dimensions, but the rest of the head seemed to bulge out behind as if blown up with a bicycle pump. At a distance of ten meters, Consuela couldn't tell in the meager light whether the beings had arms and legs; certainly they weren't easily distinguishable from the cylindrical torso and vestigial neck on which the head was balanced, as if it would fall off in the slightest breeze.

Surrounding the sawed-off figures in the center of the circles were four smaller certified copies of the original, facing inward, eyes focused on the larger Formigan. Despite the multitude, the room was soundless, nor was there any movement. And yet both Griggs and Consuela felt that something was happening. Griggs tried to catch the eye of the central figure in the circle nearest them in the reasonable expectation that he could establish communication as he had with Queen JEH, by mutual scrutiny. But the Formigan was apparently oblivious of their presence. Nor were Pat and Mike in evidence.

"Let's have a look-see," suggested Griggs, taking Consuela by the hand.

"Do you think they bite?"

"Naw. Formigans are peaceful types. They look a bit like Aunt Agatha, some of them, but there's no harm in them. If there were, we'd have known about it by now." He absently scratched his armpit.

They walked slowly together down the circles of Formigans, between the rings of light. Close-up, they were as mysterious in form and function as they had been at a distance. The large, hydrocephalic heads suggested mental activity, just as the small heads of Pat and Mike and their brothers suggested its absence. The attitude of the Formigans was strongly reminiscent of the teacher surrounded by his pupils, hanging on his words as he imparted the wisdom of the ages. If this were indeed the fact, however, the wisdom was dispensed without words, pictures or other symbolism.

They had gone for some distance when Consuela stopped. "Do you think that circle of light has any significance besides keeping the place lit up?"

"Such as?"

"How do I know? You're the scientist. I ask the questions, you provide the answers."

"Okay, ask away."

"Well, you notice that we're walking *between* these circles of light. Why?"

"Why not? We've got to walk somewhere."

She looked at him craftily. "But you haven't walked *on* the circles, *caro* Griggs. Why not—afraid you'll be burned?"

He shook his head. "If it's the same stuff as I've seen before, and it appears to be, it's absolutely harmless."

"Well, then."

He sighed, and edged his foot toward the nearest strip of illuminated fungus. His foot blotted out the light, but there was no other effect. He tried his hand.

He felt nothing—no heat, no vibration, no sensation whatever.

"Harmless, like I said."

"Good." She stepped smartly into the circle—and even more smartly right out. She swallowed. "I heard a voice."

"I didn't."

"Step in there, and you will," she assured him.

He did. And she was right. It wasn't exactly a voice, but a stream of words was now definitely impinging directly on his mind without the intermediation of sound. The Formigan's mouth did not move by so much as a millimicron. It was baffling, because the Formigan wasn't looking at him. In fact, he wasn't, on closer inspection, looking at anything at all: his tiny eyes were tight-shut.

"I'll be damned." Still looking into the face of the Formigan for some sign of life, he said over his shoulder, "Step in here a minute."

He waited for the pressure of her hand in his, as he held it out to her. There was none. He looked around, and found her regarding him with puzzled eyes. "Well, come *on*."

Her lips moved, but he couldn't hear anything.

He shouted to her. She gave no indication that she had heard. He laughed. "Well, I'll be damned," he said again. He reached over the circle, took her hand, and drew her to his side.

"What's going on?" she asked.

"Ain't that somethin'?" he smiled. "An invisible sound barrier. Sound just doesn't penetrate that circle. That's why we hear inside it, but not beyond."

"But what is it? Sounds like Pig Latin to me."

"Close, baby. That's real Latin we're listening to. We know it's Latin somehow and somehow we can still understand every word of it. Weird, isn't it? Listen . . ."

The voice droned on. After a while they realized they were listening to a recital of the life of Christ, probably one of the Gospels from the Vulgate version of the Bible, otherwise why would the recitation be in Latin?

Suddenly the voice stopped. Almost simultaneously, another began. The voice seemed different, less assured, but it was speaking—if the word speech could be applied to the mental apprehension of what was being communicated—in the same antique Latin.

"What do you make of it, Griggs?"

Griggs smiled broadly. He was in heaven. "Wait until I write *this* up. Remember the *memorialists* I was telling you about? Well, Connie, this is them—or is it 'that's they'? I don't know how they're working it, quite, but basically I think I've got a handle on the process.

"All those visitors from the outside world had tales to tell, information to impart, advice to give. The Formigans, having no other way of recording it, over the years evolved a refined version of the village storyteller. We're looking at him. These Formigans are the grotto's living memories. They have listened to the tales, compiled the information, sorted out the wisdom, and, since they are not immortal, are passing it down to young Formigans who together will form the repository of Formigan knowledge for yet another generation.

"In this chamber," he went on, savoring the thought of the history books that would have to be rewritten once he brought a tape recorder and a couple of thousand cassettes of tape down from the surface, "are the secrets of three thousand years. Do you understand what I'm saying?"

She nodded. "Of course."

"No, you don't," he said firmly. "*I* don't. It's too big for a human brain to comprehend. Look—right here in front of us is the true story of the Crusades, direct from the lips of men who battled through the campaigns. Here are the details of what happened after the Great Plague killed off one-quarter of Europe's population and the modern economic era began. One of these Formigans, maybe, has memorized the life story of someone who actually knew Leonardo da Vinci, can quote his words, tell us how he looked, describe his hopes and dreams and failures. Maybe here we can listen, in Aramaic, to the actual words of Christ, from someone who heard him preach before he wandered west, and got lost in the jungle that lies over our heads. The inside story of the Borgias, the Hohenstaufens, Charlemagne, Martin Luther—hell, the panorama of all of history, *as it really was.* Right here, Connie. Think of it."

She looked at him wonderingly. "You're something, Griggs, you know that? Who the hell cares? Why do you want to get a new version of history—to torture poor students who are having troubles enough with the old one? And what *difference* does it make? Everybody knows that people since the beginning of time were lousy, or good, or cowardly, or brave. Does it matter which was which, now they're all dead and buried? Frankly, I don't see the point in digging up their bones and sorting them out in different boxes. And that's what you'll be doing, if you start taking down all this crap on tape."

"Crap's last tape?"

"Huh?"

"Never mind." He shook his head. "Connie, you're a lovely girl and a terrific woman in bed—or out of it, for that matter—but you—are—a—moron."

"Maybe," she smiled provocatively, "but I know how to make you, the genius, sit up and beg, now don't I?"

"Woof, woof," Griggs said. "What do you say we sample some more of the goodies?"

They stepped out of the circle of light and into the one just beyond. Here the voice spoke in Spanish, a Spanish of the day of Cervantes. In fact, the voice was reciting, with many obvious mistakes and omissions, a play by Lope de Vega, doubtless dredged up from dim memory by a Spanish missionary or merchant who chanced this way.

"Wait'll I spring this on one of my linguist friends," he said. "He'll have to scrap his Ph.D. dissertation and start from scratch on the pronunciation of 16th Century Castillian. I always did think he was pulling his facts out of thin air. This proves it."

The next circle regaled them with a series of dirty limericks in upper-class British English. The series was long, profane, and very funny, despite being related in the dry and humorless Formigan monotone. They spent some time with this one. Upon leaving—the recitation was apparently endless—Griggs scratched an X next to the circle with his boot, so that it would receive his early attention on his return. For he had observed that the limericks were not only contemporary but, judging by the various accents, vocabulary and subject matter, the verses embraced five hundred years of British history, as recited by men who had lived it. They presented a view of history seldom encountered, history as seen through the eyes of wits instead of musty, book-writing, grudge-bearing drudges.

What Griggs had said about the huge chamber holding the secrets of history was literally true, as they discovered during the next few fascinating hours. They were whipsawed back and forth from century to century, eavesdropping on court life, the military camp, the ship forecastle, the monastery, the prison, the alchemist's cellar, the peasant's hut, the Battle of Lepanto, the medieval stable, and a dozen other places and happenings, including an orgy in a Greek courtesan's establishment attended by Pericles. When they finally sat down to rest, refreshing themselves from the *indki* Griggs carried in his pockets, they were emotionally wrung out from all they had heard.

"That Lydia," said Consuela.

"Yeah," replied an awestruck Griggs.

"I surely never heard of *that* wrinkle."

"Me either. Want to try it?"

"And how! But not until we get the—"

"Oh, yes—definitely. Wouldn't be half so much fun without *them*."

"Those Greeks. . . . I always wondered why we had the classics jammed down our throats in school. Now I know."

"How true. If I'd heard of Lydia before, I might have become a classical scholar instead of a lousy anthropologist. . . ."

They left each other alone with their thoughts for an interval, then Consuela said: "One thing bothers me, though."

"Shoot."

"I don't know quite how to explain it. You see, we heard a lot of history, reminiscence, data, whatever you want to call it, and it all flowed so smoothly."

"So?"

"Well, the Formigans got all these stories and information from travelers, not out of books. Yet the information and narratives we heard were *organized*. They weren't told the way people talk to each other, with a lot of 'umms' and 'aahs' and backing and filling. The stuff was—was—"

"Edited?"

"Exactly."

"And the question is—how, and by whom?"

"That's the question, Griggs, my boy."

"I'm sorry, but I don't have a clue."

But after another few hours of fascinating listening, they had not only the clue but the answer.

They were sitting in the lotus position listening to a recipe for the cure of the French disease, apparently derived from an old English herbal, when they saw the familiar forms of Pat and Mike coming toward them, dragging monstrous red stalks behind them.

At almost every circle they paused. The eyes of the pundit, as Griggs and Consuela had come to call the central Formigan to distinguish him from his disciples, would open. A look passed between him and the two guides. Thereupon Pat and Mike stepped into the circle, grasping their snakelike stalks outstretched in both hands. The disciples' heads snapped back in unison, their mouths popped open, and then almost immediately closed, as they resumed their inward-facing position. Not until Pat and Mike came to the circle in which they were sitting did Griggs understand what was happening.

Griggs and Consuela had been occupying the same circle for quite some time because the subject was the indiscretions of Louis the Pious, who didn't appear to

have been so pious, after all. The pundit had recited
his piece for an uninterrupted period of perhaps twenty
minutes. He then fell silent as each of his four disciples, in turn, attempted to duplicate his exact words.
They were not altogether successful. The general
meaning was usually close to the mark, but the nu-
ances varied from one disciple to another. Still, it was
an amazing display of memory, were this the first time
they had heard of Louis' transgressions. Griggs had, of
course, no way of knowing whether it *was* the first
time.

He decided it wasn't when Pat and Mike, ignoring
them completely, entered their circle, exchanged
glances with the pundit, then held the repulsive tentacles above the heads of the disciples and, when they
opened their mouths, squeezed into each a single drop
of fluid from one of the teatlike protuberances.

Pat and Mike stepped out of the circle, and the pundit again began his recital, from the beginning. When
he finished, the disciples, as before, mimicked his
words, but with a difference—their repetition this time
was slightly more faithful to the original.

Consuela scratched her ear. "That's the how of it,
Comrade Griggs."

"And the who, too. Pretty slick."

"The liquid improves their memory. I wish I'd had
that when I was trying to learn my opera libretti."

"You may be right," said Griggs slowly. "But my
bet is that it doesn't improve memory, but *erases* it.
The pundit recites a chunk of narrative. The disciples
try to duplicate it. They succeed to a degree, but as
they go along, they incorporate mistakes into their
playback, and with each repetition those mistakes are
reinforced. But periodically they are relieved of the
memory of their *own* recitation. But the fluid doesn't
erase their memory of what the *pundit* said: it remains
imbedded in the disciples' subconscious, so that when it
is repeated once more, the playback is improved."

"Oh, come on, Griggs!" she scoffed. "That's the
kind of tortured explanation I used to get in political

orientation classes, to explain why capitalists get rich
while the working masses bitch."

"Well, like I said," replied Griggs lamely, "it's only
a theory. My guess is that each drop erases a given
period of memory—twenty minutes, say. Or maybe it
erases the last segment recited. We'll have to find out
by laboratory experimentation."

"Meaning we need a sample of the juice?"

"Of course."

"Count me out, Griggs. You couldn't drag me back
to that cavern of clutching black tentacles for all the
diamonds in—" she blushed. "I mean, for all the rice
in China."

He patted her hand. "We won't have to. We'll take
it away from Pat and Mike. Did you notice where
they've gone?"

"Yes. Over there." She waved her hand in the direction of the hole they had made with the *emusdor*. The
Formigans were about to pass through it.

"Quick!" Griggs grabbed her hand and bolted
toward the hole in the wall. They reached it just as Pat
and Mike squiggled through, and were pulling their red
stalks after them.

Griggs grabbed one of the stalks and without difficulty jerked it from the grasp of the Formigan at the
other end. "Go on through and hold onto them," he instructed Consuela. He was beginning to doubt whether
he could find his way around the vast subterranean
kingdom after all. So long as they had Pat and Mike,
though, they could always get back to Queen JEH's
cavern. From there they knew the escape route to the
world outside.

Consuela did as she was bade. Griggs stayed behind
and took the cap off the canteen which Consuela had
tossed him from the other side. With *indki* in abun-
dance, they no longer needed the canteen for water. In
the dim light cast by the hundreds of circles, he raised
the red stalk and gently squeezed it. It was soft and
pulpy, like a fully charged sponge. A thin stream jetted
from one of the teats into the neck of the bottle. It was
easier than milking a cow. When the canteen was full,

Griggs capped it. Grease pencil in hand, he pondered
on what to name his find. Finally he wrote: "Nepenthe
juice." That was shorter than "Forgetfulness Fluid,"
and considerably more elegant.

Squeezing through the hole in the wall, Griggs found
himself again in the company of Pat and Mike, in the
negligent grip of Consuela, whose strong right hand
held their spindly arms in a firm grip. They didn't
seem to be offended, and were grinning just as dili-
gently during their brief captivity as after their release.

Freed, they stood expectantly, as if awaiting orders.
Griggs gave them some. "Bring us some food—something different from what we had last time—except for
the *indki*, of course."

A soft murmur emanated from Pat and Mike. They
jiggled on their tiny feet, marking time. The *guard*
caste seemed always to be moving, even when standing
still. This, Griggs concluded, was because their feet
were so tiny that movement was necessary to maintain
balance, like men on stilts, which in fact in considerable measure they resembled. But right now, he wanted
them to move in the direction of food, not up and
down.

He repeated his command, but grins were his only
nourishment. He was contemplating stronger action
when around the bend appeared a small procession, ten
tiny courtiers, their big hands extended before them as
if they were bearing laden trays. Each was filled with
fungi of types that he had not yet seen. He turned to
Consuela, who turned a little green.

"What are these things?" she quavered, edging behind Griggs.

"The new foods I requested, I guess."

"I mean *them*."

"Oh—*them*. I'd forgotten you haven't been around
whenever they brought me food. But I can tell you
this, Connie—it's delicious."

"But what *is* it?"

"Nice succulent molds, smooth and silky slimes,
marvelous mushrooms, savory blewits, tasty truffles—
things like that."

"I'm supposed to eat *those*?"

"Try them. Try them without preconceptions, and you'll think you're at the Tour d'Argent."

"What's that?"

"Some beanery in Paris, I believe."

Consuela's stomach was aching for food, but it was also doing backflips at the thought of ingesting molds, slimes, and blewits, whatever *they* were. But hunger at last overcame incipient nausea, and she selected a handful of the least offensive looking fungus of the lot, something that looked and felt like semi-cooked cold spaghetti. She nibbled it warily. It tasted like heaven, a cross between avocado and fresh celery. Emboldened, she tried one after another, pausing from time to time to drink the contents of an *indki*.

"Absolutely marvelous," she exclaimed as her hunger pangs disappeared at last beneath a small avalanche of the exotic fare. "What'll we have for dessert?"

"Here's something that looks interesting," said Griggs, scooping up a handful of brilliant yellow little pods. He popped one into his mouth. "Delicious," he proclaimed. "Try one."

She did, chewing it with gusto, and nodding agreement with his verdict.

"Strange color, though," Griggs said. "First time I've seen that particular shade of fluorescent yellow down here."

"Me too," said Consuela thoughtfully. She regarded the bright yellow buds in her hand. Her chewing slowed, then stopped. "Griggs?"

"Hmmm?" He looked up.

"Griggs," she repeated, her voice choking.

"What is it? Something wrong?"

She looked suddenly stricken.

He eased her to the ground. The courtiers came closer. "Beat it," Griggs snarled.

They did, waddling off single file, as they had come.

"Connie, what's wrong?"

"I think I'm going to be sick."

"What the hell? Everything *I* ate seems okay."

Consuela fumbled at her web belt, and removed a small green nylon packet. She handed it to Griggs, who held it up so he could read the words stenciled in black on the case. The words, in Spanish, read: "Dye marker. If forced down at sea, on approach of rescue craft, pull tab. Released dye will mark an area 50 meters in diameter, visible from aircraft up to 20 kilometers away."

"Pull the tab," she instructed.

He did. A fine powder floated to the ground. In his hand were two of the mushrooms he had been eating. He placed one of them on the powder. It was swallowed in invisibility.

Consuela and Griggs looked at each other wordlessly. Pat and Mike grinned.

Griggs had to be sure. "The pilot carried one of these?"

She nodded.

"Could be a coincidence," he said, knowing he lied.

"Sure," she said, pretending he hadn't.

But she failed. Leaping to her feet, she dashed a short distance down the passageway and let herself go, retching with great heaves of her broad shoulders.

Griggs didn't bother to go down the passageway, but vomited his lunch at the same place he ate it. That a considerable quantity of it splashed on the feet of Pat and Mike didn't bother him in the least.

Nor did it bother them. They never stopped grinning.

14

Pat and Mike hadn't run off despite the temporary indisposition of Griggs and Consuela while they relieved themselves of the mushrooms. To Griggs, that was a good sign. He was determined to get out of the grotto at once, and their presence was assurance that they were still under his control.

He hadn't been so sure, before. True, Queen JEH had promised that Pat and Mike would lead them wherever they wished to go. True, they had visited the extensive fungus farms, guided by the indefatigable Formigan soldiers. On the other hand, when they came to the cavern of the memorialists it appeared that Pat and Mike were trying to give Griggs and Consuela the slip. Unless, of course, their sealing up the entrance to the cavern with *rodsume* had appealed to the Formigan sense of humor, knowing that Griggs had a sample of *emusdor* with which to open it up again. And now, when they could have vanished with ease, Pat and Mike held back. Griggs decided that he was still calling the tune. That being so, he resolved that the time had now come to make his farewells. He could always return, with a battalion of U.S. Marines as escort.

"Let's get out of here," he said to Consuela, scratching his crotch. Somehow, his trousers seemed to have shrunk.

"I'm ready," replied Consuela shakily, wiping her mouth on the sleeve of her battle jacket.

"Take us out," Griggs commanded Pat and Mike, emphasizing his meaning with an upraised finger jabbing holes in the air.

Whether they caught his drift or not, Pat and Mike

113

responded with a muted murmur, and then turned and
tangoed off. Although the slight pause between each
five steps to regain their deteriorating balance gave the
illusion of awkwardness, they moved with deceptive
speed. Griggs and Consuela had to hurry to keep up
with them as they now entered a maze of shorter
corridors with numerous branchings. Pat and Mike
showed no hesitation in choosing which branch to take.
That their path led to the surface was apparent from
the gentle upward slope of the route nearly all the way.

Once Consuela, her eyes alert for the telltale glints
of light in the passageway, fell behind on the pretext of
removing a pebble from her shoe, and pocketed a
flashing gem of the type known as "river," a pure white
stone tinged with a prismatic blue radiance. Rising, she
dusted off her knees and scratched her itching left armpit before jogging ahead to catch up with Griggs. In
silence they steadily pushed on along the monotonous
pink passageways, their eyes on the spindly figures who
were taking them out of this fascinating, but now suddenly ominous, place. They tried to think of other
things, to keep their minds off fluorescent yellow fungus and the horror of the Formigan subhumans who
would use human dead upon which to grow their food.
Griggs saw Consuela shudder and he knew exactly
what she must be thinking.

More than half an hour had elapsed in this gradual
ascent when, as they passed a bifurcation in the tunnel,
Consuela suddenly turned back to plunge down the
path they had passed. From the corner of her eyes she
had seen a faint shimmer in the dim light down that
tunnel, and thought it another diamond. To her surprise, as she crouched to pluck the stone, the shimmer
resolved not, as she supposed, into a nugget of crystalized carbon, but silky strands of what seemed to be
human hair—white hair. The hair blanketed a stretch
of passageway, but it issued from another at right
angles to it. More damned fungus, she thought disgust-
edly, and rose to rejoin Griggs.

But he was already by her side. "What gives?" he
said.

"Oh, nothing," she answered, chagrined at having chased a will-o'-the-wisp.

"What's this?" Griggs asked, bending over and taking up a handful of the silken filaments.

"Yes, I saw that. It looked funny. That's why I—"

"It looks like hair."

"It does, doesn't it? Their damned fungus comes in thirty-nine delicious flavors."

Griggs studied the stuff in his hand. Using it as a guide rope, he followed it through the cavern entrance, pulling himself along as if he were in a boat. The hair got thicker. Now it was not only in his hand, but underfoot, a soft, silky mass that felt as if he were walking on down. He could see nothing except the luminous strip on one side of the wide tunnel, rather brighter than usual, and shaggy pillars in a long line on the left, from which the hair seemed to flow.

One of the pillars opened its eyes and spoke: "Would you mind terribly letting go of my beard, old boy?"

Griggs complied with the request, leaping straight up in the air. When he came down, each of his own hairs standing approximately parallel to its neighbors, he shrank back as far as he could against the opposite wall and peered at the talking pillar.

The pillar chuckled. "Sorry to have given you a fright, but it *is* damned painful when someone is tugging at the old chin foliage."

"What's that?" Consuela asked from the entrance, diverted temporarily by the gleam of a peanut-sized gray diamond, which she pocketed negligently, the novelty of discovery having begun to pale. "I thought I heard a voice."

"You did, young man," said the pillar. "Mine."

Consuela shrieked once, and threw herself into Griggs' protecting arms.

"Who the hell are you?" Griggs demanded.

"Ah, yes," intoned the pillar. "I'm afraid I have been a bit deficient in the matter of introductions. I forgot that although the presence of an alien has been known to me for some time, I am a complete stranger to you. Allow me to present myself—Gerald de Blac-quiere Gower, K.B., O.B.E., M.D., F.R.S. Lately of St. Buttolph's Hospital, London."

Griggs goggled inanely. For a moment, he couldn't think of anything intelligent to say to that. Instead, he croaked: "How lately?"

"Nineteen twenty-four," said the pillar of hair.

"The English campers!" cried Griggs.

"The very same. The seven gentlemen on my right and myself. I won't bother with introductions since they're regenerating just now, and are quite uncon-scious of your presence. Anyway, you'll have plenty of time for that, later on."

Griggs licked his lips nervously. "What do you mean by that, Mr. Gower?"

"*Doctor* Gower, my dear boy—or Sir Gerald, if you prefer—unless you insist on the typical American dis-regard for proper form. And the name is pronounced *Gore*, as in blood, of which I gather you have shed a substantial amount before Queen JEH's merry men brought you down to us. Pity you didn't kill them all," he remarked pensively. "And while on the subject of death, since you are the current candidate, might I have the honor of knowing whom I am addressing?"

"Oh, sure. Sorry. My name's Maynard Griggs, Ph.D. And this lady is—"

"*Lady*? Surely not. That uniform—"

"If she took off the trousers and battle jacket, you'd know she was a lady, all right."

"My very next suggestion, as a matter of fact."

Consuela regarded the pillar of hair with compressed lips, her eyes flashing sparks. "I am Consuela Millán y Gorgas, a major in the Cuban Army," she declared haughtily. "And majors in the Cuban Army don't undress for dirty old men."

"Your freedom of movement will last approximately three more hours than if you don't, my dear," he said gently, "but then, that is your choice."

"Freedom of movement, eh? I'm free to move right now, and in three hours I'll be long gone from here."

"No," he said, with infinite regret. "You'll be here among us—forever. One of the living dead."

A block of ice began to form in the pit of Griggs' stomach. "What do you mean?"

"Tell me—why are you scratching your neck, Major Millán?"

"Rash, I guess. Itches like hell."

"Yes, it does, doesn't it? Unfortunately, it isn't a rash. It is a species of fungus. The planters have impregnated you with the spores of that fungus. Soon you will be covered with it from head to foot. It will be very uncomfortable for you, and it was for that reason that I suggested you remove your clothes, since thereby the process is somewhat retarded. In any case, you will grow progressively weaker as the hours pass. The fungus buds—which look like ripe red cherries when mature—will grow and spread to cover your entire torso. Within a day and a night you will become immobile hulks, like us, unable to move from the shoulders down. They will prop you up in line—having us on our feet, you see, gives the fungus a greater cultivable area than if we were lying down—and you will become another member of the Queen JEH's fungus farm, anchored forever in what fate has decreed is to be your home port, the Hall of the Ancients."

"But *why*?" Consuela wailed. Her body was suddenly aflame with an irresistible itch, not entirely attributable to her imagination.

"No, of course, my dear—you don't know, do you?" Sir Gerald was silent for a moment. "The red fungus is the food upon which the Queen of the Formigans survives. The 'Royal Red,' it is called. For three thousand years, Queen JEH has feasted upon it, grown on the torsos of visitors incautious enough to step within reach of her guides. She—"

"Hold it, Doctor," Griggs intervened. "Queen *JEH*, you said?"

"Yes."

"The *same* Queen JEH?"

"The very same. At least, I suppose it is the same, since none of us saw her more than once. That should not be surprising, though, for the Formigans cultivate food which gives *us*, too, what is apparently unlimited longevity. Somewhere down the line to my right, you will find the living, breathing remains of Teaspes and Fyrlax, sailors of Hanno the great Carthaginian navigator, whose probable accidental infection with the red fungus began the whole dismal process of which we—and now you—are the victims. Sometimes, frequently in fact, I wish I hadn't been born a white man . . ."

"Hey! What's white got to do with it?"

"Only on the bodies of white men can the 'Royal Red' be cultured."

"Then I'm safe," Griggs exulted. "*I'll* get us out of here, Connie."

"No," the bewhiskered pillar said.

"I'm black, don't you see?"

Sir Gerald was silent.

Griggs ripped open his khaki jacket, displaying a broad chest like burnished black walnut.

Sir Gerald sighed. "I'm sorry, Dr. Griggs, but I don't see as well as I once did. I can perceive your outline easily against the fluorescent strip, but such refinements of perception as facial detail and color have long since slipped away from me. I'm truly sorry."

"Be happy, Doc. If only white men get this red fungus you're talking about, then I'm in the clear. And if I'm in the clear, I can get Connie out—and you."

Again, Sir Gerald didn't reply for a long interval. "Perhaps it would be better to delay telling you the truth, and give you another few hours of respite from what will be a terrible fate, but since you too are a man of science, I'm sure—"

"Get to it, Doc."

"You say you are black. Black men, too, are brought down into the Grotto of the Formigans. They become, like us, fungus farms. Some are living, but most are dead—generally of fright, for the Formigans, assured of an ample supply, take no measures to keep from alarming them, as they have with you."

"Alarming them?"

"The explanation is tedious."

"Then save it. Right now, tell me about what happens to blacks—you say they become fungus farms, too?"

"Yes."

"For what kind of fungus?"

"It is a sea green fungus. Quite tasty."

"You've *eaten* it?"

"It is our sole sustenance—but perhaps I should begin at the beginning . . ."

15

In an age lost in the past, long before the Pharaohs began to build pyramids, a race of troglodytes had achieved a harmonious existence within the confines of this very grotto. Their population was stable, and their physical make-up was only marginally differentiated, so that one Formigan was pretty much like another. None knew when they had descended from the jungle to the stable environment of the grotto they hollowed out below, but it was possibly tens of thousands of years earlier.

Apparently the advent of the Carthaginian sailors triggered a cataclysmic genetic event. Heretofore, a whole congeries of female Formigans had borne young. But when Queen JEH, as she was later to become, first heard the sailors' sea chanties—perhaps sung here in bravado or in hopeless desperation—a change occurred within her: she became immensely fecund. Her offspring, moreover, were far from the sensitive, frail creatures who had previously died in as great numbers as were born, but were virile and aggressive. They dis-

covered that they could dominate the young of other
Formigan mothers, and domination became the prelude
to murder—not only of their cousinly offspring, but
their mothers as well. Within a very short period, the
halls of this underground kingdom resounded to the
tramp of many feet, those of the progeny of Queen
JEH, alone.

Formigans had only two natural enemies. Against
water they were defenseless, for it seared their sensitive
skins like a corrosive chemical. But continually seeking
shelter from the torrential jungle rains had taxed their
food-gathering capabilities, so eventually they retired
entirely underground and there perfected the art of
fungus cultivation. There too they found their other
natural enemy, the *ogulg*, the only four-legged predator
impervious to their protective scent. Both enemies were
thwarted in primeval times, and the race of Formigans
multiplied. With multiplication came diversity. Instead
of each Formigan performing the many tasks of the
kingdom, individuals became specialized. How the
physical process evolved whereby the specialist castes
developed specialized bodies so as best to perform
these specific tasks was never elucidated. It could be
surmised, however, that a powerful interaction occurred between the Carthaginian captives and Queen
JEH.

Music, even oft repeated, stimulated her to prodigies
of procreation. Humans of the outside world might find
this remarkable, until they reflect on the powerful effect of music upon those to whom it is a common experience. Martial music drives men to war and to kill.
Soulful music causes tears to flow. Sensuous music
arouses erotic desire. Chamber music induces a restful
frame of mind. Rock music unleashes frenzy. Queen
JEH, unacquainted with music of any kind, responded
by delivering young at a vastly accelerated rate.

The stimulation of their music created empathy of
another kind between Queen JEH and the two Carthaginian sailors. Mental telepathy to one degree or another is too common a phenomenon to be called into
question among humankind. Generally the communica-

tion is quite tenuous—a premonition of danger, a preception of an event transpiring afar, an affinity between man and woman across a crowded room. In the grotto of the Formigans, over a period of time, perhaps many years—for the fungus that bestowed longevity was being eaten by aliens too, a subliminal form of communication between Queen JEH and her human subjects evolved: Queen JEH found that she could, at will, conjure up information from their minds. At first, the information was trivial, vague, and at the level of consciousness. As the years rolled on, however, her ability was refined. She could, eventually, dredge up from their unconsciousness events of which they had lost all recollection. Their minds became extensions of her own.

But nature makes its subtle compensations. As her ability to transfer the contents of their brains to hers was honed, and her will came to govern theirs, even at long range, her own powers of ratiocination atrophied. No longer could she recall the incidents of her past that once her mind had recreated with crystal clarity. Or it may have been that the absorptive power of her brain was limited, that there was room in it for only just so much.

Whatever the case, she began to communicate her new-won information, as she collected it, from her own mind to that of surrogates, which eventually evolved as a separate caste—the *memorialists*. Their sole function was to remember. And as they became more adept at remembering, the volume of their brain cases increased generation to generation, in Lamarckian response to Queen JEH's need. As they were fed by another caste, their need for locomotion disappeared, and in time they became simply living memory banks, incapable of reason, incapable of decision, but with a remarkable ability to soak up facts and fancies, like students in French lycées.

The process of specialization was extended throughout the colony as a product of metabolic economy, for food supplies could never quite keep pace with the burgeoning Formigan population, and the colony could therefore not afford duplication of effort.

Thus the *gleaners* combed the jungle floor for debris to be used as a culture medium for fungus, on which the *planters* cultivated strains of fungus, yeasts, rusts, slimes, molds, or other mycetozoans. The *courtiers* and *guardians* fulfilled the feeding and grooming functions of the colony. The *healers* were, in effect, the colony's antibodies, preserving the Formigans' health and well-being. The *memorialists* were the guardians of the colony's collective experience. The *minstrels* became the artistic, generative impulse. The *guards* did duty as the self-defensive instinct of the colony. And the Queen was the organizing will. No one caste could survive without the others. All were subordinate and at the same time all were supreme, for the absence of any caste's contribution meant the immediate extinction of the Formigan race.

Conceptually, as well as in practice, the Formigans constituted a single organism. Each separate function could be compared to an organ like the stomach (*courtiers*), lympathic system (*healers*), hands (*gleaners*), or heart (*the Queen*), and each individual a specialized cell. From the analogy, only one organ was missing: the brain. This had been supplied by the unlucky wayfarers who stumbled into the domain of the Formigans and became the captive gray matter of the realm. Until their coming, the Formigan race had, for the most part, subsisted on an instinctive level, at the level of the lower animals. But once the poison—or nectar, depending on one's viewpoint—of music was introduced, the entire character of the colony changed. Instead of maintaining its modest, unchanging place in nature's scheme, neither outgrowing its food supply or living room nor falling below the level of bare subsistence, the unfamiliar combinations of vibrations had set off a chain of colonial mutation. Like a cancerous growth, the queen who succumbed to the Lorelein lure extirpated her sisters and their offspring, and with a voracious appetite and fearsome fecundity spawned a multitude of young. They in turn devastated the forest cover overhead to provide food for the workers who bored hundreds of miles of tunnel—the colony's veins and arteries—merely to accommodate their numbers.

But periodically nature exacted its price. As the music lost its potency in promoting the fertility of the queen, population declined through natural attrition—accidents, epidemics no known myxomycete would combat, and predators. Many times had the Formigan kingdom teetered on the precipice of extermination, only to be saved by the fortuitous appearance of some passing white man. (It was always a white man who brought salvation, for the ancient, traditional melodies and rhythms of the Magenda d'Zondo had long since lost their efficacy.) And then the kingdom would flourish for the space of another twenty or thirty years, only to decline anew.

The most recent arrival had been a disappointment. He had come upon the scene very recently, being brought in by the guides from a Magenda d'Zondo village to which they had been drawn by the sound of music. The acquisition proved to be a Belgian lay missionary named Jean Bercque, a rather dim individual with a sanctimonious manner, a perpetual toothy, inane smile, and his tape recorder. The music lasted only as long as the player's battery. Thereupon, he appealed to Queen JEH to parole him, on his bond as a fervent Christian, to entice other, more musical white men to the grotto in return for his own release.

Queen JEH had seriously considered the proposition, but in the end refused. The man had a shifty, hand-washing manner, and her surrogate brains told her emphatically he wasn't to be trusted, either to return or with the secret of the Formigan grotto, whose security would be hostage to his silence. In the end, Jean Bercque was consigned like all others to the tomb-like Hall of the Ancients. He was that man on Sir Gerald's right, the one with the short hair . . .

Griggs examined the man in the faint light. His hair and beard were short—only about two feet long. That accorded fairly well with the length of hair a man would grow—at the usual rate of a centimeter a month—in five years, if this indeed was the Belgian missionary who had disappeared about that long ago from the Magenda village. The missionary's body, exposed in its entirety where the others were blanketed in hair, seemed to be covered in vesicles the color of raw hamburger from his narrow shoulders to his bare flat feet. His mouth, now that Griggs looked closely, was moving, but no sound issued from between the lips.

"What's he saying?" Griggs asked Sir Gerald.

"God knows," sighed Sir Gerald. "God knows—literally. I suspect he's praying. He usually is, but for what, I cannot imagine, since he goes in mortal fear of dying, the only fate the rest of us pray for. But he'll never die, poor fellow. After all, he is fed regularly, his bodily wastes are removed to provide a medium for various fungi, he is never hot or cold, and from the looks of him and his pietistical airs the absence of carnal pleasures is no hardship. He's been a very dreary addition to the assemblage, I am bound to say."

Griggs looked down the row of old men. The white-haired columns of men reminded him of a long line of Lots, turned to salt. "Still" he reminded Sir Gerald, "you've got lots of other company to talk to." Once again his blood warmed at the thought of hearing the history of three thousand years, from the lips of those who lived it.

Sir Gerald sighed again. "Not so much as you'd think. You see, while our facial nerves have remained more or less intact over the years, since they have no part in the process of the growth of the Royal Red Fungus, our bodies have been useless to us since a day or two after we entered this accursed place. First the feeling of pain subsided—that was a blessing, after the terrible itching—then absolute nothingness, as if we were modeled in stone.

"Well, of course, that prevented movement, so that if we wanted to wander down the line to indulge our curiosity about our fellow inmates—as indeed we, even as you, did—we couldn't do so. Then too, after about a hundred and fifty years, the facial nerves and muscles atrophy in their turn. Usually it's the sense of touch that goes first. As a medical man, I attribute that to a complete lack of stimulation, for as you've doubtless observed there is neither a current of air here nor the slightest variation in temperature. Then the senses of smell and taste depart, for the same reason, no doubt. After having supped for five or six years on the identical fungus on which you've lunched and breakfasted, it's a wonder these senses respond even that long. Hearing and sight then go, as I say, anywhere up to the age of about 150, and we are left in darkness. I myself, by this reckoning, have another 65 years to go."

"So that's the end, then?" Griggs said.

"Oh, dear, no. In a way, it's only the beginning. You see, Dr. Griggs, one is alone with one's thoughts after that, for many, many years—many lifetimes. As a scientist, you are doubtless aware that epithelial cells can regenerate, at the most, some forty times. This is what limits an individual human lifespan. Since these are the cells upon which the Royal Red Fungus grows, however, and this fungus itself acts in some mysterious fashion to switch off or override the genetic instructions that limit this regeneration, the body cells continue to reproduce without cessation. They thus provide what is, I'm afraid, as close to an eternal nutrient for the fungus as nature can contrive.

"Brain cells are, as you are also aware, nonregenerative. When a brain cell dies, it's dead. On an average, in the healthy human being some 100,000 brain cells die daily, a minuscule proportion of the body's 100 *trillion* cells. Simple computation demonstrates that the brain should be able to outlive the rest of the body by some centuries. I have made that computation thousands of times, and I judge that at least a certain small portion of my brain will be functioning 450 years hence, before I become a total vegetable. It is not a comforting thought."

Grigg's throat felt very dry. He stared at Sir Gerald with horrible fascination. The man was discussing his future with a certainty that mortal man had never been able to do. He *knew* he'd be alive four more centuries, able to think and remember. He *knew* that even after the last thought slipped away from him into the abyss of nothingness, his body would live on, providing food for the obscene Queen JEH. And still he spoke calmly, as if he were reading a paper to the Royal Society. Griggs, who never for a moment doubted that he would be able to extricate himself and Consuela from the grotto, experienced a feeling of infinite sorrow for this aged husk, whose only crime had been to sing earthy limericks in the Congo jungle.

"So you see," Sir Gerald went on, "I have not been able to participate in the absorbing discussions which I, like you, envisioned, once my fate was made clear to me. Down the line to my right is a former first-mate of Sir Walter Raleigh. He was a page to Queen Elizabeth I as a boy. His life was a tapestry of action, thought, suffering, intrigue, passion, and ambition; his brain is now but a shred of that bold fabric. Further along . . . but why tell you—you'll know soon enough."

"But how do you *know* all these things, if you haven't been able to communicate with these people?"

"Oh, that's simple enough. The contents of their brains have been transcribed into the robotlike memories of the *memorialists* with whom, through the mediation of the will of Queen JEH, we share a common consciousness. What they knew, I know, down to the last detail. I know the very words used by William the Conqueror when he damned his vassal Engelbert the Celibate for cowardice and set him adrift in a rudderless bark, only to be captured by a Portuguese coaster which foundered on the reefs in the Bight of Biafra. I know the invocation given by the Bishop of Chartres at the consecration of his great cathedral. I know the perversions of the concubines of the second son of Tamerlane, the color of the eyes of the beloved of Frederick the Great of Naples and the Two Sicilies, the names of the Spaniards who died on Cervantes' ship at the Battle of Lepanto, the fate of the Roman soldier who nailed the feet of Christ to the cross. Ah—what do I *not* know . . ."

"Do you know any reason why we can't simply walk

out of here?" said Consuela, bringing the old man back to the present.

"Yes," he said gently. "Several."

"One will do."

"Very well. First the time element. You think you can retrace your way out. After all, you have been to the surface once and you remember, you *think*, the route, so—"

"How the hell do you know that?"

"I've told you—I am a cell of the living organism. I know what Queen JEH knows, as she knows what I know."

"You mean she knows what is going on right now—she knows what we're saying?"

"Most assuredly."

"But you say her will is yours?"

"That is correct."

"Then why," pursued Consuela, "does she let you tell us all this?"

"Because she is rather an evil old party, really. She gets what little joy there is in life for her matching wits and wills with people who stray into her web. She allows me to talk freely, lets us give you any information you want, secure in the knowledge that you will be unable to profit from it."

Consuela and Griggs looked at each other uneasily in the dim light. As if on cue, both scratched—Griggs his crotch, Consuela her armpit.

"Take off your clothes," counseled Sir Gerald. "The itch will not be so severe. Of course, after a few years, you'll scarcely notice it any longer anyway."

Griggs unbuttoned his shirt. After a slight hesitation, Consuela followed suit.

"Look, Dr. Gower," Griggs said firmly, "we're getting out of this place. Believe me—we are. And we'll be back, but before we go there are a few things I want to know."

"I too had your overweening self-confidence the day I arrived here," Sir Gerald said sadly, "but look at me now. Still, miracles happen, though I suggest you don't confide yours to me."

"Don't worry—I won't. . . . A while ago, you said something about 'measures the Formigans took not to alarm me.' What did you mean by that?"

"Ah, yes. Well, you see, it was crucial that you remained calm. I suppose you know that while leading pigs to slaughter, it is essential that until the moment of their killing they be kept calm and unafraid. Fear stimulates the production of lactic acid and various hormones in the porker which, after death, causes the meat to turn watery and become unfit for human consumption. Now, it was discovered here long ago that white men who became alarmed upon being confronted with Queen JEH and her minions produced a noxious strain of the Royal Red Fungus. And the more frightened the captive was, the less palatable the royal food. Sometimes, indeed, it is virtually useless, as in the case of my colleague Jean Bercque. He was so terrified that, ever since, Queen JEH can choke down his strain of Royal Red Fungus only when the production of the rest of us is in short supply.

"You may not realize that a fresh Royal Red Fungus donor, such as Señorita Millán, is an essential complement to the new music in the generative process. The fungus produced by the Ancients suffices for her daily rations, but it apparently lacks the vital juices a fresh donor supplies. Then too, such veteran donors as Teaspes and Fyrlax, despite regular feeding, are inevitably declining as producers. You mustn't imagine that autocar manufacturers in the life we left behind are the only ones with production problems."

"Okay, but where does the music fit in? How does that work?"

"I'm afraid you have me there, my dear Dr. Griggs. For many years I have been attempting to fathom this mystery. I have formed some tentative conclusions. You understand, naturally, the phenomenon of resonance—the crystal goblet shattered when the soprano hits G above high C. Perhaps this is part of the answer. It may be that the enormously complex vibrations of music somehow affect the regenerative organs of Queen JEH, stimulating them to action. In one of his lucid moments, Brother Bercque here has mentioned that in America there is—or was—an expression current connoting beneficial effects. 'Good vibes,' a truncated form of 'good vibrations,' he said it was.

"I believe that music provides the good vibes which Queen JEH requires to perpetuate the race of Formigans. You may well ask why the same vibes don't maintain their efficacy, to which I would answer, what vibes do? Does one's wife excite a husband after forty years to the degree she did on their honeymoon? Does a politician's promise, oft-repeated, carry the same conviction? Can you thrill to Schubert's *Unfinished Symphony* today as you did when you were fifteen? Of course not. And that, I believe, may be the explanation for Queen JEH's need for fresh music: the old tunes simply fail any longer to stimulate."

As he spoke, Consuela removed her jacket. Her amazonian breasts were covered with tiny welts, as though the skin had been pricked with a pin.

"You will be a welcome addition to our group," Sir Gerald said wistfully. "What a shame we didn't meet before I came on that wretched safari. On the other hand, you weren't born then. . . ." He sighed.

Griggs, who had removed his trousers as well as his shirt on Consuela's cue, scratched his head, as much from puzzlement as from the itch of the fluorescing Sea Green Fungus. "There's something I don't understand: Queen JEH let Consuela go."

"She did."

"But she could have stopped her."

"Yes and no. Queen JEH could have stunned her—as she did you with what, for want of a better term, I can call her olfactory weapon. But that would have frightened her, and her usefulness as a Royal Red donor impaired."

"Well, then, why didn't it frighten me?"

"Ah—that was because she assessed, correctly as it turned out, that the spirit of scientific inquiry would conquer any temporary fear you might have."

"Still, there were other ways to handle her. She couldn't very well have gotten out, after all."

"That's where you are very much mistaken. Once you were rested, Dr. Griggs, you and she together were more than a match for the *guides* who opposed you. You could have killed them with your bare hands, then simply walked out as, indeed, you did. There was no way to stop you."

"Then why can't I do it now?"

"Because you're weaker now. You cannot overwhelm the *guides* any longer."

"I doubt that I ever could—there must be millions of them."

"There were, once. But not for many years. The ones you have seen are all that are left. Until you came upon the scene, the colony was slowly dying out. Your advent and your music have saved it. Soon your—that is *your*, Señorita Millán—Royal Red Fungus will restore the Queen to health and procreativity. Once again the galleries of the grotto of the Formigans will swarm with young. If only you had not come," he said in a grief-laden voice, "then we would have all been able to die, at last."

"You really *want* to die?" Consuela said.

"I'll remind you of that question, a hundred years from now," the old man said.

Griggs was about to ask another question, but thought better of it. If it was true that the Formigan kingdom was in reality but a single organism, it would be foolish to seek a hint on how to escape from the old Englishman. Though he would have by now thought of a hundred ways, he would scarcely reveal them to Griggs so long as his will was dominated by that of Queen JEH.

"We're on our way, Dr. Gower." He paused. "I wish I knew what to say."

"There's only one thing left to say, my boy," Sir Gerald chuckled mirthlessly: "Good-bye."

16

Pat and Mike were waiting for them in the passageway outside the Hall of the Ancients. They were marking time, their tiny feet barely breaking contact with the ground, jiggling in place as if they were treading eggs without wishing to break any shells.

Griggs thought he detected a difference in their fatuous grins. Consuela confirmed it.

"They're *knowing* grins," she said.

"Yeah, but they don't know what I'm thinking. . . . Take us back to Queen JEH," he commanded, "and if you lead us astray, I'll kill you."

"Oh, sure—that'll frighten them," Consuela mocked.

"It will," Griggs assured her. "Dr. Gower said their numbers are dwindling. They're Queen JEH's only defense. She can't spare any more losses. Besides, what has she to fear from us?"

Pat and Mike observed this colloquy and, as if they had communicated it telepathically to Queen JEH and received an affirmative response, they turned and danced down the passageway. "That's the ticket," Griggs encouraged them, but he held Consuela back as she was about to follow. "Let them get well out of ear-shot. I think we can still get out of here, but it will take a bit of luck."

Consuela, scratching her torso more frequently now, as they followed the Formigan guides in the distance, didn't think it would work. On the other hand, she had nothing better to propose. Furthermore, she was beginning to feel the first telltale signs of fatigue, which Sir Gerald had promised would soon consume her. She held Griggs' hand and let him pull her forward.

Griggs said: "Why don't you give me that pistol belt and shed those pants? You can travel faster without them."

Consuela shook her head. Though she was beginning to despair of ever escaping the grotto of the Formigans, she determined to hang onto her diamonds, which would now fill the palm of her hand, come what may. And in her weakened condition, unless she had a pocket to carry them in, they would soon be scattered and lost. "Feminine modesty," she alibied.

"Suit yourself," he said, scratching his thigh. "Anyway, don't give up hope. In a couple of hours we'll be out of here, having a good hot bath—and other things . . . . We've *got* to get out of here," he added with grim-lipped determination. "Do you understand what we've seen? Do you realize that never in the history of natural science has anyone been privileged to see what we have seen and experienced in the last two days or so? Goddammit—we're *going* to get out of here, and I'm *going* to publish it all, and be the most famous goddamned anthropologist in the whole goddamned world, do you hear?"

She heard, but the words rang empty.

"And the beauty of it is, the whole thing fits together."

"What do you mean by that?" she said listlessly, just to keep her mind off her morbid thoughts.

"My research. The ritual. The whole damn thing fits."

"I don't know what you're talking about."

He laughed. "Sure you don't. I forget, you don't know about the research I was doing." And he told her how he had come to be in Africa.

"But what's that got to do with the—what did you call it—the ritual?"

"That's right, the Termite Reincarnation Ritual." His eyes took on a faraway look as he shuffled like a sleepwalker along the dim-lit passageway. The bobbing figures of Pat and Mike were well ahead, and gaining slightly. "I only saw it once, but—" He shuddered.

It had happened on a night of the full moon. His

Magenda d'Zondo maid-of-the-month, a full-bodied
lass with primitive hungers, had crept out of his bed as
he lay there, seemingly asleep, but actually considering
ways to revive himself so as to be up to the next round.
She made no reply to his sleepy query whether something was amiss, nor to his next comment, to the effect
that as long as she was up, bring him a beer from the
fridge. Instead, she had glided out of the house like a
black ghost, ignored the retracted gangplank, and vaulted nimbly to the ground. Griggs, who had got up
groggily to follow her as she headed for the door,
watched in horror as a spitting cobra reared in the
moonlight not a meter from the spot where she landed.
Yet, uncharacteristically, though poised to strike, the
cobra did not eject its stream of venom at her eyes, but
recoiled sharply and slithered away into the darkness.

That was Griggs' first intimation that strange doings
were afoot. Pausing only to pull on his boots, he
sprinted after her. It was a mile or so down a jungle
path to the village. At the high wooden palisade
around the settlement, he stopped and put his eye to
the crack between two palings. Inside, the entire population of the village was milling about in the moonlight,
as silent as death, without apparent aim or purpose,
like so many ants around spilled sugar. But even as he
watched, his face pressed against the wooden uprights,
order began to emerge among the aimless horde.

The blacks slowly collected in two masses on either
side of the *nganga,* a circular low-fenced pit about four
meters in diameter and two meters deep. The *nganga*
contained the principal source of ready cash for the
Magenda d'Zondo—the vipers, mambas, cobras, vine
snakes, and adders which the tribesmen collected to
peddle to the agents of zoos and antivenom laboratories
in Kinshasa who passed through the area every fortnight. But on this moonlit night the natives were collecting something else.

Themselves.

At first, in the dim light that filtered through the foliage, it seemed to Griggs that everybody had fallen to
their hands and knees as if worshipping a heathen idol,

or maybe looking for somebody's lost contact lenses. Then the writhing mass gradually compacted, shrank, and began to grow.

Upward. In an eerie silence that the heat and humidity of the jungle night made almost palpable, taking shape before his eyes were two human pyramids, one on each side of the snake pit.

Dark figures clawed and scrambled their way to the top of the heap, and were in their turn submerged and pressed down by others who clambered over the mass of bodies, as the mound of humanity grew ever higher. Half dazed by the spectacle, and not even faintly aware of its significance, Griggs didn't notice at first that the pyramids were not symmetrical. Ever so slightly, they leaned toward each other, arching over the edge of the black pit with its poisonous, crawling horrors.

Now movement on the lower layers of the pyramids had ceased, as though the suffocating pressure of the bodies above gave those below no room to breathe, but still the pyramids of human flesh ascended toward the leafy forest top overhead. The pinnacles gradually bent inwards, until finally they met to form a human corbeled arch over the *nganga* below. The crest of the arch was some seven meters above the snake pit, and barely the thickness of two bodies, but for a moment the immobility of the human bodies that constituted it gave it the illusion of stability, as if it had been hacked out of granite.

As Griggs marveled, successively, at the physical toughness, intuitive organization, indifference to danger, and appalling stupidity of the Magenda d'Zondo, it suddenly dawned on him that he was witnessing in human guise the work of the tribe's termite totem, the *Macrotermes natalensis*. This termite builds bridges across seemingly impassable chasms by constructing cantilevered arches of tiny pebbles and soil particles, cementing them together with droplets of excrement which they eliminate as needed, sometimes laying a blade of grass between the columns to support the lintel. Was this a demonstration of the power of the soul of the white ant, their totem, which had chosen this moment and this means to command the energies and destinies of their human incarnations?

Griggs never heard the answer to this self-addressed question. For suddenly the human arch collapsed, tumbling into the obscurity of the *nganga* the bodies of no less than a dozen of the fittest Magenda—for only the fittest could have fought their way to the top of the swaying pyramids. The bodies fell without so much as a whisper, and plummeted with a swift succession of sinister splashes to the bottom of the muddy pit.

Instantly, the human columns collapsed and dissolved as the survivors hurried away into the darkness of the jungle, never looking back.

It was all over—whatever *it* was.

Griggs walked slowly back through the dark forest to the camp, deep in thought. Nor was his disquiet allayed when the girl failed to return, and the next day the villagers disclaimed all knowledge of her, as if she had never existed.

Only after many months among them did the meaning of the savage rite become clear, and then only by the most indirect of evidence. The Magenda d'Zondo, he had discovered early in his researches, ritually devoured great quantities of roasted termites, a common African specialty, on occasions of rejoicing—marriages, the death of enemies, the birth of sons, the declaration of war. Harking back to his readings in psychology, Griggs concluded that the ritual he had witnessed was an expurgatory ceremony. In it they expiated their tribal guilt for eating their totem by periodically allowing other crawling things to devour *them*. And in mimicking the most remarkable feat of termite intelligence, the construction of freestanding arches, they had guaranteed that the best of the tribe—those who had the strength to mount to the top of the pyramids— would be the sacrificial victims of communal expiation. With this end in view, the Magenda nicely balanced considerations of religion and economics: the snakes had to be fed, for only healthy specimens were bought by the itinerant traders, bringing income to the tribe as a whole. Thus the dead bodies of their brothers attracted ants by the million and were devoured by them. And in turn, the insects were consumed by the snakes, which became fat, sleek, and desirable in the eyes of the roving snake merchants.

It was what Griggs considered one of his more elegant bits of theorizing, a splendid edifice built on a few firm facts. The only trouble, as Griggs, now in the depths of the Grotto of the Formigans realized, was that it was totally false.

What impelled the Magenda to build living pyramids was a mystery that he would perhaps never unravel. But the fate of the victims was now clear: their bodies were the main supply of nutrients for the fungus which the Ancients were fed. Once the Magenda fled to the jungle at the conclusion of their barbaric ceremony, the guides would emerge from the darkness and claim the bodies. But what of the poisonous reptiles, he would be asked. He had the answer to that, too: the repellent odor of the guides, exuding the noxious, overpowering formic acid smell, would drive the snakes to the farthest corner of the pit while the guides carried away the bodies. The disappearance of the bodies without a trace would, the next morning, confirm the Magendas' belief in the supernatural power of their rite.

"Isn't that a hell of a story?" Griggs exulted.

Consuela Millán y Gorgas found Griggs' story of the Magenda ritual sickening, and she said so. Not only was there a lot too much about snakes—the mere *thought* made her shudder—but the gory details reminded her that both of them were destined to be living fungus farms for the Formigans. Worse yet, if what Dr. Gower had told them was true, she herself would be fed on the fungus that fed, in turn, on Griggs.

"Don't let it happen, Griggs," she whimpered, suddenly seizing him and holding him tight. But the contact proved comfortless: the rubbing of her fungus against his felt like the rough tongue of a steel rasp on her flesh.

"Don't let what happen?" he said, his mind still wandering among the green pastures of celebrity that would be his when he published his findings, first in learned journals, then in the newspapers and magazines, and finally on television shows throughout the world, which would besiege him for interviews and first-person accounts.

"Anything."

"You've lost me, honey."

Consuela released him. "That's what I'm afraid of, Grigg. Losing you . . . and me."

"Forget it," he soothed her. "We're going to be all right."

"No."

"Listen—you remember saying something to me about a tape recorder—you wanting to record my *F* above high *C*?"

"Yes," she responded listlessly. He was always going off on tangents. What did tape recorders matter now?

"Where is it?"

"In the helicopter, I guess."

"Any tapes with it?"

"Of course. I have *Don Giovanni* complete, and—"

"Batteries?"

"I put them in last week."

"Great!" Griggs smashed his fist into the open palm of his other hand, and winced from the pain of abrading his fungic knuckles. "Great," he repeated less exuberantly, through clenched teeth.

"What's this about the tape recorder? What possible use can it be?"

"I'm going to make a deal with Queen JEH: I'm going to trade her *Don Giovanni* for our lives," he lied. For a moment, he was tempted to tell her the truth, to give her a reason to hang on. But thinking it over he decided that the secret might be pried out of her by the canny old queen, condemning them both to an eternity of suffering. She'd know soon enough what he had in mind.

"How?"

"You'll see. But one thing: I'll do all the talking."

Consuela sighed. "Okay, Griggs. That's what you do best." She smiled wanly. "*Second* best."

They had been following Pat and Mike with dragging steps, almost losing sight of the Formigan scouts as they danced ahead with undiminished speed. With Consuela, the *rallentando* was undisguised fatigue, both physical and from the numbing knowledge of her approaching fate. Griggs only pretended. His muscles had the strength and elasticity of the champion sprinter, but to simulate exhaustion was an important part of his planned deception. Fortunately, by the time Pat and Mike disappeared ahead, they made the last turn into the large cavern in which Consuela had been set upon by the Formigans in an attempt to sterilize her, and thus avert an invasion of baby-blue helicopters. From here, they knew their way to Queen JEH's lair.

The Queen was waiting for them, malicious eyes beaming.

You thought you could escape Queen JEH? she glowered.

Maynard Griggs shuffled his feet and shook his head in a reasonable imitation of the abashed black, caught in the act of stealing a watermelon. "Hell, I wouldn't do that, Queen," he said, speaking aloud. He wanted to be sure Consuela would follow what he was about to say.

You lie.

"Well, yes—at first," he admitted. "But after I talked with Dr. Gower, I saw it was futile to try to get away."

Completely.

"But there's something I don't understand."

There are many *things you don't understand.*

"It's about the Magenda," Griggs pressed on. "You take them dead. Why?"

If they're dead, they do not need feeding. And as you know now, the Magenda are as numerous as we Formigans are few.

"But you won't be few if you have enough music to start your reproductive processes going full blast again."

That is true.

"Do you think the music we've provided will do the trick?"

Queen JEH paused. Doubtless she was mentally consulting her counsellors, the Ancients and her memorialists, who would remember how much music had been required in the past to start her regenerative juices flowing.

There is a sufficiency.

"A sufficiency," Griggs mocked.

Yes.

"What if there isn't *quite* a sufficiency? Your whole Formigan race will die out."

Queen JEH was silent.

"There's a way of making sure," Griggs suggested.

Queen JEH replied instantly: *How?*

So, thought Griggs triumphantly, Queen JEH *wasn't* all that sure that the music they'd provided would do the trick. He had her.

"I can get you more music—a *lot* more."

Get it.

Griggs wagged his finger at her. "Uh-uh. We make a deal first."

What is the deal?

"I want to go on living. I know it won't be much of a life, but it'll be better than dying."

Living is not possible for black-skins in the realm of the Formigans.

"Racist, huh? Well, you'd better *make* it possible, Queen, or there won't be more music."

Queen JEH was silent once more. For a long time she didn't speak. Griggs wasn't deceived by the silence. He knew she had already decided, but wanted to lull him with false hopes. He was certain she would agree, then kill him after the music was played.

Very well, she said finally.

"Now you're talking," Griggs said with evident satisfaction. He went on briskly, "Now, then, here's what we're going to do. . . ."

Queen JEH listened without interrupting. When Griggs had finished, she asked a few questions, to which Griggs had answers rehearsed and ready.

It is agreed. But the female stays here until you return.

Chagrin, anger, conciliation, and resignation flashed across Griggs' countenance in rapid succession. All were spurious. He felt, indeed, an elation born of the assurance that he had taken Queen JEH in completely.

He'd show the old bitch.

17

The Sea Green Fungus kept rubbing together between his thighs, which felt as though they were studded with corkscrews. But Griggs kept moving, although at a slower pace, calculated to give the impression, on his return, of utter exhaustion. By then, he hoped to have just enough energy to make good the escape whose details he was even now reviewing. Up ahead Pat and Mike fox-trotted toward the buried helicopter.

Griggs had no idea how far it might be. When he and Consuela were floundering about in the forest above, lost beyond all hope of extricating themselves from the maze of intersecting paths, they must have covered eight or nine miles in all. If the mileage had been in a single direction, he would have to give up hope right now, for they would never have the strength to reach the helicopter's subterranean pad once he had delivered the helicopter's radio to Queen JEH. On the other hand, if they had been going around in circles, in the usual manner of people who have lost their bearings, the route might be quite short, perhaps no further than a mile. He fixed his mind on that possibility, and consciously excluded all others. Life was too short to allow depressing thoughts to disturb one's calculations.

One calculation, clearly impossible, was to work out and commit to memory the route they were taking. Unlike the way to the surface he had already reconnoitered, this was no single passageway, but a system of intersecting, interlocking tunnels which defied reduction to an order he could remember. Every hundred meters or so, the tunnel would split into three or four, one going upward, another swinging at a sharp angle to one side, a third turning back on itself. It reminded him of the Los Angeles superhighway system, navigated blindfolded. Never had he felt so lost.

A little desperately, he focused his ruminations on the enchanting possibility that they *would* escape the grotto of the Formigans after all. The next step would be to find medical attention and get rid of the unspeakable affliction with which the Formigans had infected them. That might not be easy. Fungal infections, he knew, are often resistant to even the best medical treatment, and those with which he and Consuela were cursed might prove to be quite unknown to medical science. But, ever the optimist, Griggs felt sure that someone, somewhere, would have the cure for them.

There had to be a cure, indeed, for otherwise how could he present his unprecedented scientific discoveries to the world? He didn't think for a minute that life could be so perverse as to let him stumble upon the most astounding race of semihumans ever conceived by the mutations of a capricious nature, only to still his voice when he was at the point of revealing its secrets, its very existence.

Visions of distinguished professorships, chairs of natural science, medals and awards, honorary citizenships, freedom of cities and the adulation of awe-struck students—preferably female, nubile and willing—chased themselves through his mind as he, in turn, chased Pat and Mike down dim tunnels and around sharp corners that seemed to go on without end. But there was an end, and after what seemed to him a fairly short trip, considering his condition, they reached it.

The tunnel suddenly opened up like a flower. There, squatting before him, as though in a clandestine hangar awaiting its repair crew, was the Cuban helicopter. The main rotor blades, twisted like arthritic fingers, were bunched together on the side opposite the entrance, their axis barely touching the ceiling, Griggs noted with satisfaction. Shards of glass from the shattered cabin bubble crunched underfoot as he walked toward the pilot's compartment to see whether anything inside had emerged intact from the crash.

Caked dried blood liberally streaked the instrument panel but, as he clambered in and eased himself into the pilot's seat, Griggs noted that the instruments themselves seemed undamaged. In the dim light cast by the omnipresent phosphorescent fungus, Griggs searched for matches or other means of illumination. In a side pouch he found it—a flashlight. He switched it on.

Pat and Mike shrank back as if doused with cold water. Griggs grinned. So the Formigans couldn't stand bright light. Good—that would be another weapon to cover their getaway. He turned the beam away from them into the interior of the cabin. The radio he sought was to the right of the pilot's seat. The power line had been severed in the crash, but the panel lights went on when he activated the power switch. He sighed with relief. The auxiliary batteries were still working. This far beneath the surface of the earth the radio would never pick up a signal, but the point was that the set *looked* alive, and the crackle and hum that issued from the speaker added to the illusion. He switched the set off, disengaged the lugs that anchored it to the floor, and lifted it out of the cabin.

He now inventoried the interior of the cabin in detail. In the passenger's seat pocket he found the cassette recorder Consuela had promised. With it were half a dozen cassettes. He inserted one, turned the volume low, and switched it on. Faintly he heard the engaging strains of a Mozart symphony. He removed the cassette, put in another, and *sotto voce* tested its recording capability. It worked fine.

As he methodically went through the contents of the cockpit, Pat and Mike kept their distances, their eyes averted from the flashlight's glare. Under the pilot's seat Griggs discovered a first aid kit and two hand grenades in a wooden box. He was far beyond first aid, but the hand grenades might come in handy. He put them in a leather map case and slung it by its strap over his shoulder.

He climbed down from the cockpit and summoned Pat and Mike. They danced up to him.

"Take it away," he said, pointing to the radio.

They grasped the radio as they apparently grasped his meaning, and with an effort that strained their rubbery arms, lifted it out of the cockpit. Without a backward glance at Griggs, who slung the leather map case over his shoulder, they struggled to the entrance of the cave and into the tunnel beyond.

It heartened Griggs to observe the effort they had to expend to carry the heavy metal case, while at the same time trying to preserve their equilibrium. With their own concerns to occupy them, they'd have no time for him. That was essential because their sensory organs were merely extensions of Queen JEH's own. If he said something the Formigan soldiers could hear, *she* could hear it too, and by means of telepathic control bend their actions to her will. Similarly, they doubtless transmitted the pictures that formed on the retinas of their bulging eyes to Queen JEH as well. That had inspired him to spray the flashlight's rays liberally around the cavern to keep them—and Queen JEH—so to speak, in the dark.

Griggs gave Pat and Mike a good head start, and then began counting his steps. At the first turn in the passageway, he pressed the *record* button and flicked on the power switch. Into the microphone he whispered: "One six six, right turn sixty degrees." On he walked, eighty-two steps to the next bend in the passageway. "Eight two, left turn 120 degrees," he confided to the tape.

Pat and Mike appeared oblivious of the chronicling of their passage. Though they never seemed to tire, they showed the strain of carrying a heavy metal object between them by the two wire handles: their gait, interrupted as usual by a slight hesitation after each five steps, was as clumsy as that of short men on tall stilts.

But if they moved with diminished vigor, so did Griggs. He wondered if he would have the strength to get back to Queen JEH's lair, and then to lead Consuela out of it. He plodded forward, itching from head to foot, at each turn in the way down whispering the information by means of which he hoped to find their way back up again. . . .

Consuela Millán y Gorgas, alone with the Formigans under the baleful eye of their queen, had long since begun to despair of ever seeing Griggs alive again. His plan of escape was sound enough, but he had visited the Hall of the Ancients too and should have been impressed as she was by the knowledge that there incarcerated were dozens of living reminders of the futility of trying to get out of the grotto of the Formigans alive. She scratched her crotch furiously and decided that she could no longer stand to wear trousers. She shucked them off and reveled in the brief respite her nudity provided. It wasn't precisely nudity, to be sure: she was blossoming with the Royal Red Fungus to a depth of nearly half a centimeter over her entire body. Only her face and the soles of her feet seemed to be unaffected. Otherwise, she had somewhat the appearance of a smallpox sufferer at the most virulent stage of his affliction, except that the protuberances were a bright red. She thanked God she didn't have a mirror. It would have been more than she could bear.

Standing first on one foot, then the other, Consuela tried to give birth to constructive thought. But despite the fact that she was alone—Queen JEH's probing eyes had blinked out the minute Griggs left—among the multitude of Formigans, she found the task impossible. For one thing, the minstrels were in full voice, bouncing off the high cavern ceiling the very arias she had sung earlier, and the noise was deafening. For another, the appearance of the various castes of Formigans wandering in and out had long since lost its novelty, but it remained a distraction. So far as she was concerned, they were all a species of animal not far removed from the ants and termites whose formic-acid smell continued to assail her senses.

One thought served to sustain her. It was the thought of the expression on Griggs' face when—if—they got out of this dreadful place, and she showed him the diamonds she had collected for them. Delighted consternation? Delicious surprise? Overwhelming relief? More likely he would experience a combination of all those pleasant emotions when he realized that not only did she intend to share this treasure (and by implication, what she hoped was an even greater one—her future) with him, but that the sojourn beneath the jungle floor had not been a complete waste, after all.

But the diamonds were in the pocket of her trousers. She couldn't possibly put them on again—they felt as if they were lined with sandpaper. Nor could she put the diamonds in the shoulder bag crowded with test tubes and plastic envelopes. The bag might be lost during their escape, or spill out the diamonds if they had to run for it.

She took the gems out of her pocket and counted them. They were eleven: black, gray, green, blue, and brilliant white, ranging from the size of an acorn to that of a robin's egg. If they managed to escape at all, she thought to herself, it would be within the next few hours. And that meant that if nature took its usual course, she could recover them intact within two to three days. Experimentally, she popped one into her mouth and swallowed. It went down easily. Another followed, and another. . . .

She had crushed an *indki* between her teeth and was savoring the fresh lemony flavor of it when she heard his voice:

"*Consuela—hey! Can you hear me?*" The shout came from beyond the mouth of the cavern. Because of the singing of the minstrels she couldn't judge how far down the tunnel he was.

The minstrels fell silent. Queen JEH's eyes were staring into hers.

Tell him to come.

"Tell him yourself, you obscene old gut bucket," she flared back.

He cannot hear me.

"Oh."

Tell him to come, Queen JEH repeated.

"Hey, Griggs—fatso says for you to come on in," Consuela yelled.

"Not a chance," came the response, from just beyond the entrance. "She hasn't tried it on you, apparently, but I can tell you this: she can flatten you like a laser beam. Sort of sets your throat on fire, just by giving you the evil eye. Tell her I'm not having any."

Consuela told the Queen, who did not reply.

"You can also tell her that if Pat and Mike try to sneak the radio off once more, I'll smash it. And that's the last music she'll ever hear."

Consuela passed along the message.

He has the music, but I have you, she told Consuela.

Griggs, his anger rising, yelled back: "If she thinks she can stall until the fungus puts us down, she's mistaken. I'm the only one who can operate the radio."

And you will give me the music?

"Listen," said Griggs.

Griggs had already switched cassettes in the player, which he placed on the ground behind the radio. Now, kneeling before the radio panel, he switched on the power. The panel lit up. His eyes fixed upon it intently, with his other hand he unobtrusively turned on the cassette player and very slowly raised it to full volume.

Music flooded the chamber.

"See how it works?" Griggs said, switching off the two machines simultaneously.

Pat and Mike grinned.

He called out to Queen JEH: "You've heard the music. Now, send out the girl."

18

She was totally naked except for the tuberous growth of Royal Red Fungus that covered her body from just below her jawline to the soles of her feet. Instead of walking, she hobbled, with feet wide-spread to minimize the painful rubbing together of her thighs. Her canvas bag with the fungus specimens weighed heavily on her right arm, held away from the body, as did the web belt festooned with first aid kit, whistle, sheath knife, canteen, and a plastic bag filled with *indki*. Regarding Consuela in her present state, Griggs wondered how he could possibly have found her irresistible only hours earlier. He turned away—the sight was too painful.

"Let's move," he said to Consuela, picking up the tape recorder and setting off at as brisk a pace as he could manage with the matted growth of fibrous fungus, which looked like Shredded Wheat but felt like Brillo. "I'll do the navigating, you watch our rear."

"Better than watching *your* rear," she assured him. "You look like a roll of green barbed wire."

Griggs switched cassettes once more, then turned on his tape recorder and rewound the tape to the last segment. He engaged the *play* button and listened to his voice saying, "One two zero, descending, left turn one eight zero degrees."

"Think it'll work?" Consuela enquired.

"Our road map?" Griggs shrugged. "You better hope so. It's the only thing that *can* work down in this labyrinth. How many miles of tunnel did old Dr. Gower say the Formigans have built over the past three thousand years—'hundreds?'"

"Something like that," Consuela replied listlessly.

"Well, if we didn't have this little jim-dandy, we could wander around for months without ever finding the exit. Always assuming, of course, that we weren't about to collapse from fatigue from carrying this load of fungus. . . . Okay, here's the first turn: 180 degrees to the left—I mean *right*. I've got to remember to do everything backward: if it says right, that means left. If it says descent, it means ascent. Don't let me forget."

"All right."

The two grotesque figures, one blood red, the other deep green, both bloated and stiff from their coating of fungus, staggered on. Griggs counted 120 paces before making a turn, again to the right, in obedience to the instructions he had recorded. So far, it was all proceeding according to plan. If only their strength would hold out, they'd be in the clear. Once again, he diverted his mind from his pain-racked body by focusing it upon the acclaim that awaited his report to the world. It would be a sensation. Sensation, hell—it would be a triumph.

"Griggs?"

Griggs didn't reply. The voice had intruded into his daydreams. If he paid no attention, it might go away.

"Griggs!" came the insistent voice again.

"Present and accounted for, Major."

"One thing I don't understand."

"Only one?"

"Why the hell are we going *this* way?"

"Because I've *been* this way, that's why. And also because this way leads to the helicopter, which is buried just beneath the surface. We dig through a couple of feet of earth, and we're home free."

"Home the hard way," she said testily. "Maybe you don't remember, but I've already been out of this place, once. I just walked up this sort of circular ramp, and in half an hour or so I came out in the jungle. No problems."

"Yeah," said Griggs.

"Yeah what?"

"Have you looked behind us lately?" Griggs asked.

"Sure I have. That's what you told me to do, and I've done it."

"And what have you seen?"

"Nothing."

"Exactly. And do you know why?"

"No."

"It's because Queen JEH *knows* you have been up that nice, uncomplicated ramp, and came back the same way. Why would we look for any other way out, with that route staring us in the face?"

"Stupid me." She tried to laugh, but the laugh, filtered through her suffering, came out a croak.

"You just didn't have as much time to think about it as I did," Griggs said gently. "Sure—she's deployed her remaining Formigan guides in that area of the grotto, waiting to pounce on us. It's the obvious thing to do. In our weakened condition, it wouldn't take much to wrap us up, either."

"You don't think maybe she's got a few hidden along the route we're taking, do you?"

"I doubt it. She's strapped for manpower. Even in our present state, we could slaughter enough of them to put their survival as a Formigan race at risk. Besides, I've been up and down this particular stretch of country twice in the past couple of hours, and I never saw a soul except Pat and Mike. . . . No, I think we're safe, although it won't hurt to keep your eyes peeled."

"It wouldn't hurt to get my whole *body* peeled."

"Patience . . ."

For what seemed like hours they toiled ahead, carefully following the taped instructions. Sometimes they seemed to be going in circles, and at others, downhill rather than up. But Griggs knew how deceptive gradients can be without a standard of visual comparison, and he forged stolidly forward with complete faith in the accuracy of the direction he had committed to tape.

Their discomfort had reached the point where each step was agony, even without the additional weight of their various burdens. Time and again Consuela implored Griggs to allow her to discard the bag, which weighed ever heavier. She pointed out that, once they were out of the grotto of the Formigans, they could come back prepared for every contingency and harvest the fungi the bag contained a dozen times over. Curtly, Griggs told her to save her breath: he hadn't gone through all this to return to the surface empty-handed. For all he knew, the music they had left behind might fail to set in train the Queen's regenerative processes, and by the time he could organize a return trip they might find nothing but corpses.

"It could be worse than that," Consuela said grimly.

"How so?"

"The corpses could be ours."

Her tone brought him up sharply. "Trouble?"

"Plenty," she said. "They're right behind us."

Griggs halted and swung slowly around. His sheath of fungus didn't permit any faster reaction. He felt as though he were encased in a suit of armor filled with angry fire ants.

The Formigans were following, all right. The passageway behind them was filled with bodies pressing forward. They were at least fifty meters away yet, but closing the gap rapidly with their familiar five-step-pause-five-step-pause shuffle.

"Do something, Griggs!" she entreated him.

Griggs unhooked the flashlight hanging on the web belt and flicked it on. He filled the tunnel behind them with a burst of light.

The effect was magical, as if a transparent wall had suddenly been thrown up before them. The leading guides stopped abruptly, and tried to retreat, but the momentum of those behind them flung them forward. Their balance was broken, and they tumbled, all in a heap, a score or more of them. But the flashlight's beam was as devastating as a flamethrower, and hurriedly scrambling to their feet, the guides fled back the way they had come.

Griggs handed Consuela the flashlight. "The moment they show themselves, give them a blast of light."

"Right."

They plodded wearily onward.

It wasn't that she actually *saw* anything. It was more of a *feeling*, as though the tunnel was shrinking behind her. She had dismissed the thought as the consequence of fatigue and fear when she turned around to determine if the Formigans were keeping their distance. But the next time she looked, certainly not more than ten seconds later, it appeared that the tunnel had almost swallowed itself. She reached forward and touched Griggs. He jumped as though burned with a branding iron. "Jesus!" he cried, "Be careful."

"I think they're coming again."

"Can you see them?"

"No," she said tremulously, "but I can smell them."

Again Griggs swung ponderously around. "What the hell!" he blurted. The last turn was more than a hundred meters behind them. Yet behind them now was a solid wall. Sudden terror seized him. Thrusting Consuela aside, he snatched the hand grenades from the leather map case, pulled their pins, and flung them in quick succession down the tunnel. Griggs threw himself to the ground and with a leg scissors brought down Consuela on top of him. As he rolled over, shielding her body with his own, the grenades exploded.

Fragments of shrapnel whizzed by overhead, and they were showered with bits and pieces of Formigan flesh, warm and adhesive. The concussion made their ears sing, but at least the smell of cordite overwhelmed the acid stink of the massed Formigan bodies. For a moment, Griggs felt, the menace had been held at bay.

But Griggs didn't wait to see. He rose on limbs as stiff as fence posts, lifted Consuela to her feet, took the flashlight and pistol belt and shuffled on down the passageway, dragging her behind him. He was beginning to feel extraterrestrial, with his flesh-crawling shroud of green fungus, now unmistakably alive, a million tiny worms feasting off his body, the transistor tape recorder in his left hand, the flashlight in his right, the pistol belt looped around his neck.

Consuela was even less appetizing, except maybe to

a hungry Queen JEH, covered as she was with thousands of angry red fungal carbuncles.

They staggered on. At the next bend in the tunnel, Griggs glanced back for some sign of pursuit. There was none. Furthermore, the tunnel behind them presented its normal, unshrunken aspect. He pondered over the strange illusion that the tunnel had been closing in behind them. No explanation came to him, however, until he dislodged a vagrant shard of what seemed to be black vinyl from his forearm. That provided the germ of an answer.

Since the Formigans had proved photophobic, the flashlight was as effective against them as a machine gun. Repulsed, the Formigans doubtless communicated their dilemma to Queen JEH, who mobilized the intellectual resources of the Ancients and the memorialists to find a quick solution. It would probably be another fungus, of course, Griggs concluded. He remembered having seen one that would fit the bill, and had even taken a spare sample from the fungus farm for his collection: a black fungus of uncertain function that grew in long sheets from the ceiling of the cavern where it was cultivated. The sheets, though paper thin, were opaque and as tough as vinyl. What the Formigans used it for, Griggs couldn't guess. But obviously they had provided themselves with a large disk of the fungus to use as a moving shield both protecting themselves from the light and providing camouflage for their advance. It was this moving shield that had given the illusion of the tunnel swallowing itself.

Griggs grunted with quiet satisfaction for having solved another problem. Thinking about it had kept his mind off his other worries, such as that which now faced him as he turned a bend in the tunnel—and came face to face with four Formigan guides. He hoped they would attack, and the moment he saw them he yanked the trench knife from its leather scabbard on the belt and waited for them to commit suicide. He could dispatch them in short order, and the more dead now, the fewer to contend with later. But they wisely retreated in good order, dancing backward with effortless ease as he hacked away, unsuccessfully trying to cut them down. He followed them down one passage, around a turn to the left, and up another, futilely carving arabesques in the air with his knife.

He wondered why they were provoking him. They weren't hurting him, certainly. And they weren't interfering with his forward progress. If anything, they actually were serving as guides, leading him toward the—

Toward the *what*? That last turn he'd made blindly, following the Formigans instead of obeying the taped instructions. What if they were leading him—not to the helicopter but down the garden path? In fact, why *would* they lead him to the helicopter, which they and he knew lay only a meter or two below the surface— and freedom?

Griggs sheathed the knife and switched on the tape recorder. He heard his voice say: "Eight two ascending slightly, left turn one sixty degrees." He flicked the switch to "pause," and himself paused in thought. Yes, they had covered about eighty-two meters in the section of tunnel they just left; and yes, the tunnel was descending, as it should be, going the other way. Then the turn. Yes, it was about 160 degrees, and to the left, just as he . . . hold it, Griggs! he said to himself. The turn was to the *left* going *down* into the grotto, so it had to be to the *right* going back *up*. He blinked leaden eyes at the Formigans, marking time just out of his reach.

"You sonsofbitches," he growled. He flashed his light on the guides, and they fled up the tunnel as if doused with molten lead.

"What's going on?" Consuela said, bleary-eyed. Her words were slurred, her tongue thick. She sounded as if she had just knocked back three quick martinis. She plodded after him, dragging her feet as if they were encased in divers' boots. Plainly, she couldn't last much longer.

"It's nothing," Griggs said in a voice stronger than his conviction. "Wrong turn."

"How much farther is it?"

"Not far."

"How *far*?" she wailed.

Griggs turned his light on the cassette in the recorder. To his astonishment, one of the spools was nearly empty. That meant that, in truth, they were nearly at the end of the road, if they could only find the right road. "We're close. Believe me, Connie, we're *real* close. Don't fold up on me now, baby."

She didn't reply.

But he wasn't listening anyway. They had returned to the last bend in the tunnel. It was, indeed, an angle of about 160 degrees. He walked over to the smooth wall at the point where the tunnel would have cut back on itself, had it been going to the right. "Hand me the bag."

She handed it over, mutely.

Griggs fumbled through it, found the test tube labeled *emusdor*, and uncorked it. He dipped his little finger into the test tube, extracted it smeared with the slime, and drew a large circle on the wall. He waited thirty seconds, and leaned against the center of the circle. With a crash, a disk of blue ground as thick as the safe door of a small-town bank fell in a cloud of dust into the passageway beyond.

"I'll be damned," Consuela gasped through dry lips.

"Come on."

Like robots, they strode stiff-legged through the opening, over the disk of earth, and onward.

Griggs was going on instinct and reflexes now. The tunnel ahead was empty, but it seemed a million miles long. Each step was more painful than the one before, and every ten paces or so they had to pause and rest before pushing on. The armor plating of fungus each carried grew heavier as it sucked nourishment from the muscles beneath. Only grim determination not to fall victim to the Formigans kept them moving ahead, but they were failing fast. Griggs knew that only minutes remained before they would be too weak to resist the guides' onslaught.

They turned the bend that Griggs knew would be their last. They simply could not go any farther—not a single step. But they didn't need to: they had arrived.

There, before them, was the helicopter.

And there, too, were the Formigans.

Unless Griggs was very much mistaken, these would be the sole surviving guides. In the dim light, they didn't seem too numerous. No more than fifteen or twenty, he guessed, a number which, had he been in robust health he could have annihilated in a matter of half a minute, leaving a trail of broken legs and smashed skulls behind. But he knew that even two or three guides would now, in his dilapidated condition, be a match for him. Then, suddenly, he remembered his flashlight. He really must be on the verge of blacking out, he reflected, for it was grasped in a death grip in his right hand. He switched it on.

The Formigans stampeded toward the opposite wall, through an opening which Griggs now perceived they had made there. In the blink of an eye they had disappeared.

Griggs croaked: "I'll go first." He clambered woodenly up the shattered shell of the helicopter, using the bent fuselage and gaping cockpit window brackets for a foothold. Standing on the cockpit, he reached down for Consuela's hand.

"Look out!" she cried, and Griggs straightened just in time to switch on the flashlight and catch the Formigan phalanx boiling out of the entrance shoulder to shoulder. The beam sent them rushing pell mell back the way they came.

Again he reached down, as feeble as one of the Ancients, and slowly drew her up beside him. "Almost clear," he mumbled. "Give me the tube of *emusdor.*"

Consuela drew the cork. Griggs inserted his finger, described a circle on the ceiling where the disk of earth would fall clear of them, and was recorking the test tube when he felt a soft hand on his leg. "You bastards just won't learn," he growled through parched lips, and again switched the flashlight on. It blazed for a moment, then blinked out.

He shook it viciously, but the light didn't come back on. He cursed the Cubans who had made it. More soft hands tugged at his ankle. He flung the flashlight down at the mob of *guides* who were now swarming up after them. "The *indki*," he shouted.

With her last reserve of strength, Consuela reached into the plastic bag and pulled out a handful of the small soft globules. Griggs grabbed them and shoved one in his mouth. Biting down on it, he sprayed the liquid on the Formigans. They released him and fled, as if the flavored water were a corrosive acid.

But the retreat was only temporary. Each time Griggs braced himself against the rotor to smash his fist against the disk of earth, which was presumably ready to fall at the slightest touch, the guides returned, and he'd have to pause to spit another *indki* at them. Only one *indki* remained when he at last swung his fist against the spot he had circled with the *emusdor*. A dozen hands were grasping at his ankle as the disk suddenly fell with a shuddering thud on the Formigans directly below.

The disk of earth wasn't all that fell.

Above them, in the circle of darkness, their first view of the world outside the grotto of the Formigans in what seemed like months, the Great Rains were falling. The water came down in torrents, in such mighty quantities that Griggs and Consuela felt as though they were climbing up into a waterfall. They staggered clear, walked a few steps, and collapsed. . . .

The Formigans who had survived the onslaught of Griggs and the earth fall were eleven in number. They were the last of the Formigan guides. When they saw the torrential rains pounding down, they retreated to the inner passageways out of harm's way. Their collective consciousness, in tune with that of Queen JEH far below, sought guidance.

It came. They were to await the end of the downpour, which would soon come. Judging by their condition, the victims wouldn't move for some time. The growth of the fungus would furthermore, make them steadily weaker. Once the dry veld had drunk up the tropical shower, it would be safe for the guides to venture out. They would bring in the victims. Queen JEH ordered it.

The Formigans waited.

And, as wise Queen JEH had promised, the rains finally stopped.

19

The insane laughter of a hyena at close hand awakened Griggs from the stupor of total exhaustion. Vaguely he recalled having crawled and clawed his way out of the hole in which the helicopter was interred, but he couldn't remember much of anything else. It took a while for him even to realize that he wasn't alone, and in pitch blackness, with rain pouring down upon him. He gingerly probed the area around him with an arm grown fat with the green fungus. His hand encountered the yawning vacancy in the ground, and pulled hastily back. He dragged himself a few meters away in the mud and again swept his arm in a semicircle. This time his hand brushed the disgusting rubbery knobs which told him that he had touched Consuela, though on what part of her body it was impossible to tell. She didn't stir. With sudden anguish, he feared she might be dead.

The scuttle of feet in the muck in which he lay brought him painfully upright into a sitting position, his arms raised defensively before his face. For an instant, he thought it must be the Formigans, perhaps protected from the rain by sheets of the gray vinyl-like fungus, intent on dragging him back to the living grave they had prepared for him. But a flash of lightning dispelled that horror—and revealed death in another guise, even more imminent: the gaping mouth of a hyena, its canines as long as his finger, not more than half a meter from his face.

Griggs was literally paralyzed with fear. He had been in Africa too long to believe the conventional tale that hyenas are cowardly scavengers which skulk in the vicinity of kills left by lions. On the contrary, as he had seen with his own eyes, hyenas are daring and desperate predators, and lions are not too proud to dine off *their* leftovers. At the moment, however, the distinction was academic, for it appeared that the hyena had finished his reconnoitering and was preparing to sink his fangs into Griggs, who could do no more than dumbly await his fate. He gritted his teeth and turned his head away.

But the bite never came. Instead, a wave of the familiar acidic Formigan stench surged out of the hole and washed over them, and the lightning that lit up the countryside a moment later revealed no sign of the hyena. The beast's departure was only marginally reassuring, though, because the odor clearly indicated that the Formigans were close, and ready to seize him. He knew that the instant the patter of rain ceased, the patter of little feet would begin, and he would be enveloped in soft little hands bearing him down into the grotto of the Formigans, into hell on earth. And he was too weak now to resist.

But the Formigans didn't come—yet. Slowly the stink dissipated, and Griggs was left to conclude that the sharp senses of the guides had detected the presence of the four-legged interloper which would steal their prey, and sent up a cloud of its own particular brand of animal repellant. As long as the rain persisted, the Formigans would wait in the dry sanctuary of their tunnels. But Griggs knew that these tropical deluges cease with as little warning as they begin. It was time to move on.

Summoning up his last reserve of will, he heaved himself forward to his knees, swayed there like a palm tree in a high wind, and fell full-length on his face. He groaned with pain and frustration, the rain hammering down on his bare back. He knew then there was no es-

cape. He could only count the minutes helplessly until
the rain stopped. Then the Formigans would come to
reclaim their human aphids. There was no point in
fighting any longer. He sank into a resigned semicon-
sciousness, lulled by the drumming of the rain on his
bare body.

And then the rain stopped, all at once, as if a faucet
had been turned off. Griggs, momentarily reviving, said
a silent prayer but, not being a church-going man, was
not surprised when the prayer wasn't answered. For
now he heard them coming—tiny, rapid sloshing
sounds, like a handful of pebbles flung in a shallow
puddle. He felt their gentle caressing of his body, as
they probed for handholds on the obscene matted
growth that obscured and rounded every feature. The
acid stink, temporarily washed from his nostrils by the
rain, came back with vivid pungence. He was tugged
this way and that. Griggs didn't bother even to open
his eyes. What for—to witness his humiliation in their
grinning faces? Besides, it was too dark to see anything
but the shadows of cloud against the stars.

Still they worried his pain-racked body, like puppies
playing with a rag doll. Griggs found himself wondering why they didn't simply hoist him aloft as they had
done before, in the jungle, when they bore him and
Consuela off to the depths of the Formigan kingdom.
And as they continued to pull at him, the answer
came: *because there weren't enough of them.* He had
apparently slain just enough of them to make the load
of his body too heavy for the survivors to lift, failing
which they were hauling first at one leg, then the other,
nudging him an inch at a time toward the hole above
the helicopter. Once they'd dumped him and Consuela
inside, they'd roof over the hole as they had before and
haul him back to his alotted row in the fields of fungus
by easy stages.

Well, not if he could help it. He felt an emptiness
beneath his right foot, and with a superhuman effort
kicked loose the tiny hands and rolled away in the opposite direction, coming to rest on his back. With each
successive tug forward, he shoved himself back with his

heels. Manpower—or Formiganpower—was on their side, but time was on his. He had no idea what time of night it was, but if he could just hold out until the first rays of dawn appeared in the eastern sky, he would thwart them, for the sun was an even greater enemy of their hypersensitive skin than the rain. In a dream, he battled on.

When the sun rose, after a small eternity, the Formigans had already departed. They must have seen the false dawn in the sky and realized that the struggle had been lost. They trooped single file back to the helicopter cavern, quickly applied *rodsume* to the aperture, and vanished from sight. But before they departed, they left a legacy: a ring of stink around the two humans sprawled in the mud. This was an obvious warning to beasts of prey to avoid the victims whom the Formigans intended to reclaim when night again fell, for by then the remaining strength of the victims would have evaporated in the rays of the burning sun.

The sun was already at its zenith when Griggs heard a low moan from Consuela, calling for water. He was parched himself, despite the liberal quantity of runoff that had trickled into his mouth during the downpour. But he had no water. Even if he had, he lacked the strength to give it to her. The hours passed in leaden procession, as he faded in and out of consciousness. From time to time in his delirium, he imagined himself being dragged toward the pit and his feet began feebly to churn the drying mud. But mostly he lay still, eyed from afar, by soaring vultures waiting for the twitches to cease and their feast to begin.

A sudden rise in the wind, until then but a steady, gentle breeze, signaled his torpid mind that soon night would fall and the Formigans would come back for him. Slow anger rose within him and he cursed aloud.

To his astonishment, his voice rang out sharp and clear. He opened his eyes and closed them again, scarcely able to believe that the movement of the lids did not cause him excruciating pain as they had since the fungus had loosed its poisons throughout his body. He moved his hand experimentally, then his arm. No pain. He looked down, expecting to see the disgusting green mat of interlocking strands of fungus. Instead, the fungus had become a pale yellow-green. Desiccated by the sun's infrared rays, and already scaling off in spots, patches of new pink skin were beginning to show. Taking a deep breath, Griggs heaved himself to his knees, then to his feet. He was unsteady, but he stood!

"Connie!" he yelled, exulting.

A weak groan was her only response. He turned toward the sound.

She was sprawled in the mud, now caked and cracking in the sun. She was a sorry spectacle, but she was alive. And she was certainly in better shape than when he had seen her last. The Royal Red Fungus had retreated, as though growing in reverse. In place of angry red carbuncles, crowding each other for a place on her body, were pale pink bumps, not unlike the nipples of women of the Slavic races. It was evident that she had undergone an ordeal every bit as harrowing as his own, and Griggs thought that perhaps she had like himself given up hope. Obviously she had not realized that the fungal infection that afflicted her had receded beneath the healing rays of the sun.

"Wake up!" he commanded, bending over her and massaging her neck.

"Ouch!" she exclaimed, her eyelids flickering. "That hurts."

"Good," Griggs replied, heartened by the reaction. If she could complain, there was hope. "Come on—get up." He gently put his hands under her arms, and slowly lifted her to her feet. He had already spotted the Range Rover not more than a hundred meters away, at the margin of the jungle just where she had left it, seemingly eons ago. He urged her, with faltering steps, in that direction. Already the sun had sunk like a stone below the horizon, in the disconcerting manner of African sunsets, leaving a smear of red and purple across the western sky. Sooner than he would like, it would be dark, and the Formigans again on the prowl. Before then, he intended to be well away from the accursed spot, back in the sanctuary of his cabin with its gasoline lantern, locked door, and lockerbox full of weapons. "Move!" he ordered.

Halfway to the Rover she stopped. "Water!" she gasped, motioning feebly to her mouth.

Griggs, who had slung the muddy specimen bag over his shoulder and fastened her web belt around his waist before setting out on the 100-meter safari back to the Rover, reached automatically for the canteen. He shook it. It was about half full. In a few minutes they'd be back at the cabin, he computed, with enough water to swim in. He unscrewed the cap and held the canteen to her lips. She drank greedily, but he pulled away the canteen before even half the liquid was gone. "Easy does it, Connie," he cautioned her, screwing on the cap and dropping the canteen back in its canvas pouch. "Too much all at once will make you sick."

She looked at him vaguely and shook her head. Her eyes dropped to her own nude, muddy bare body, covered with frightful pink bumps. She shuddered. She looked at Griggs again, seemed about to speak, then shook her head once more and allowed herself to be pulled along toward the Range Rover.

In another two minutes, taking slow, painful steps, they reached it. Griggs helped Consuela into the vehicle. He tottered around to the driver's seat and climbed in beside her as gracefully as if all four limbs were encased in plaster casts. It was getting dark, and from the rain clouds collecting in the west the jagged edges of lightning flashes hurtled toward the Earth.

Thick fingers turned the ignition key, and after several futile whirrings the motor sprang to life. Griggs put the vehicle into gear and eased it around in a tight semicircle, heading for camp. "Just in time," he remarked grimly.

"Time for what?" Consuela asked with narrowed eyes.

Griggs pointed to the rain clouds, and then with his thumb back over his shoulder. "They'll be following us, but with that rain coming down, they'll never get to first base."

"Yes, that's true," she mused. "Thank God for that."

"You said it. I'm going to stand under that rain so long it'll take fifteen towels to dry me off. I'll never knock rain again so long as I live, seeing as how we'd be dead if it weren't for that downpour last night."

She regarded him strangely. "I don't understand."

"No, I guess you wouldn't. You were unconscious the whole time."

"I guess so." She shook her head and winced. She had a monstrous headache. "But what's that about the rain?"

"Well, the storm saved us, that's all. They were looking for us, trying to rope us in. But it looks as if God called the game on account of rain."

"Oh, yes, of course. It would, wouldn't it—the poor visibility and all."

"That, and the smell."

"Smell?" She sighed. She could hardly think, let alone talk.

"The formic acid smell. They must have squirted some of their stink around us when that hyena showed up to measure me for his dinner plate. One whiff of it, and he was off like a shot."

"You've lost me again," she said indifferently, not giving a damn one way or another. All that had happened was so wild and unbelievable, she preferred to terminate the discussion until she could take a couple of aspirins for her aching head and give her brain a chance to sort things out.

"Never mind," said Griggs, sensing her mood. "I'll tell you all about it later."

She nodded.

Griggs maneuvered the Rover around the spur of jungle in low gear to spare them the discomfort of jolting across the ruts and potholes. He had the headlights on now, and kept his full attention on the trail ahead. He didn't notice the sidelong looks Consuela gave him from time to time. Even if he had, he would not have been concerned. After all, they had been through an astounding adventure in the past—how many days was it now? Small wonder that she should regard him speculatively trying to determine where he fit into the life that their refusal to give up had reclaimed.

Just ahead, the camp loomed in the headlights. Griggs drove up the hill in low gear and stopped half a meter from the veranda. He switched off the engine, sighed heavily, and stepped across to the reassuring familiarity of the veranda—*home*!

He held out his hand. She took it, and together they walked into the house. Griggs pumped up the lantern and lit it. Hung from its hook on the ceiling rafter, the lantern cast a light bright enough for Consuela to see Griggs clearly for the first time since he had brought her back to consciousness at dusk.

He was a horrible looking creature. His curly hair was matted with mud. He was naked, with a bristly suit of pale yellow-green extending from his neck to the soles of his feet. His eyes were tired and bloodshot. A six-day growth of beard streaked with dirt and sweat covered the lower half of his face. He looked like nothing and nobody she had ever seen. He looked like a goddamned Martian.

She looked him in the eye. "I've got a question," she said sternly.

"Only one?" he said with a weary grin. "I've got a million."

"Mine first."

"Yes?"

"Just who the hell might *you* be?"

20

Griggs was depositing the canvas specimen bag and the web belt with its various appendages on the table when the question hit him like a bucket of ice water. He flinched, and the web belt fell to the floor. Automatically, he reached down to pick it up. His hand fastened on the canteen, the canteen which held—he felt a draft of frigid wind across his bare back—the *nepenthe juice!* Suddenly the import of her words became perfectly clear.

Her memory had gone. She didn't know who he was. He straightened and turned to face her, trying to remember that he was, to her, a complete stranger.

"The name's Griggs—Maynard Griggs."

"I see," she said stonily. "And what are you doing bare-assed like this? And where the hell are *my* clothes? Also, what is that damned outfit you're wearing? And why do I—"

Griggs raised his hands. "Hold it. One thing at a time. You've been sick. Both of us have. Rare jungle disease. Happy to report you're recovering. There aren't many after effects, though I've heard tell that the disease you have sometimes affects the memory."

"Nothing wrong with *my* memory, friend," she snapped.

"So you say. Can you remember your name?"

"Certainly. I am Consuela Millán y Gorgas, pay—" She stopped suddenly, fear and cunning erasing the indignation in her eyes. Just in time she remembered who she was, and realized for the first time who this strange man in front of her must be.

"You were saying?" Griggs prompted. "Pay what?"

"Uh—ah—*painter*," she stammered.

"Painter?" The black man seemed amused.

"A portrait painter, actually," she said, wishing she were better at improvisation. But this would do, for the moment. She wore no uniform, so the green-suited stranger could not possibly know she was an officer of the Cuban Army. And since he was speaking American English, the odds were that, despite his grotesque appearance, he was an American. Americans believed anything. "Yes, that's right—I'm a portrait painter."

"What's a girl portrait painter doing wandering around naked in the jungles of Zaïre?" he asked, with skeptical eyes.

"*Zaïre?* This is Zaïre?"

"That's right. Where did you think you were?"

Consuela hadn't the slightest idea where she thought she was. "That explains everything," she temporized. "Everything."

"Not to me."

"Well, you see, our plane—I was in a plane—it had a—a—"

"Navigation failure?" Griggs suggested.

"Right!"

"And then it crashed?"

"How did *you* know?"

"And you were the sole survivor?"

"Listen—"

Griggs said: "What kind of plane was it?"

"A DC-3," she said promptly.

"And it crashed in the jungle."

"Yes, we must have." She couldn't remember the crash. He was right—she couldn't remember *anything*. The last thing she recalled was Rivera the helicopter pilot wisecracking about the two of them shacking up in Kinshasa. After that—a total blank. They must have been shot down. Probably by a heat-seeking missile fired by an American advisor of the Angolan resistance groups trying to subvert the legitimate, Cuban-backed regime. Despite the strange pale green disguise he wore—probably a new kind of jungle camouflage—this man Briggs exactly fit the profile of the mercenaries they had been so often warned against: American, black—to blend in with the natives—young, tough and smart. If only she could remember what had happened. . . .

But Consuela could reconstruct the events, at any rate. The American CIA men heard the approach of their helicopter and shot it down. But then they must have been unable to locate it in the jungle at night, and called in one of their trackers—Briggs here—and sent him to look for it, wearing his camouflage uniform in case he ran into Cuban troops. Meanwhile she, dazed and confused, her clothing ripped off by jungle thorn bushes, instinctively sought to get back to headquarters on foot, only to be intercepted by the black tracker.

This didn't explain the terrible rash covering her body, an infection so severe that it couldn't have appeared overnight. Which meant that she had probably been wandering around in the jungle, semiconscious, for days. And this black man had found her and now was pretending to believe her story about being a survivor of a crashed DC-3 in order to disarm her and win her confidence. And when he had it he would worm out of her the site of the crash, the cargo, and the mission.

Well, he wouldn't learn a thing from her. Her duty was to get back to headquarters and aid in the recovery of the helicopter, Rivera, and the payroll. But until she was able to travel, she'd have to play along with this Briggs, disarm his suspicions, catch him unaware. Then, like the good soldier she was, she'd kill the mercenary without mercy and find her way back to base. They might even give her a medal. . . .

"We need something to drink," Griggs said. He went to the fridge and produced two cans of beer, very warm, the butagas bottle having long since been exhausted. As he opened them, he reflected that perhaps her inadvertent drinking of the *nepenthe juice* which he had put in the canteen was not an unalloyed tragedy. The accumulating horrors of their escape from the grotto of the Formigans had come close to unhinging her mind. One day he'd tell her what really happened and she'd have a good laugh about it. But for the present, it was better that he didn't make any mention of the termite people. Her pathetic attempt to cover up her flight from the Cuban Army he excused philosophically on the ground that she was too ashamed to admit that she was a deserter and a thief. By and by, though, the whole story would come out, Griggs would assure her that it didn't make a damn to him, and they would then be free to plan their future together.

The second can of warm beer made Consuela aware of just how exhausted she was. Her eyelids felt like iron shutters. There were a lot of questions unanswered, but the question of her safety with this man never entered her mind. If Briggs was soft-headed like most Americans, he might actually have swallowed her story about the DC-3 crash, though she doubted it. If he was soft-headed, like a lot of other Americans, he would never think of molesting her, a "defenseless" woman. She chuckled at the thought as he handed her a third beer.

It put her to sleep. Her last recollection was of Griggs lifting her out of the wicker chair, which he had thoughtfully lined with a towel to ease the discomfort of her affliction, and carrying her to one of the cots at the end of the room. He did so with ease. There were muscles beneath that camouflage uniform. As she drifted off to sleep she wondered whether he would make love to her. It didn't matter one way or the other, but she thought it might prove very uncomfortable for them both under the circumstances. But instead of rough hands, she felt the gossamer breath of the mosquito net being lowered around her and tucked in under the mattress.

Griggs was as exhausted as she was, but responsibility kept his eyes open long enough for him to take a few sensible precautions for the night. First he locked the house's single door and secured the wooden shutters over the windows. Anytime now, an hour after sunset, the wind would freshen and thirty seconds later the rain would start pelting down, to continue until shortly before dawn. The rain should stop the Formigans, but in case it didn't, then the door and shutters would. Still, to be on the safe side, Griggs filled the lantern reservoir to its brim and raised the wick to cast a brilliant light over the room. Should all else fail, he provided himself with his Smith & Wesson .38 from the aluminum trunk where he had locked up his weapons. He checked that the cylinder was fully loaded, and slid the pistol under his pillow.

Griggs glanced at the bag of fungus, slime, mold, and other mycotic specimens beside the table, and decided they'd keep until the morrow. The *nepenthe juice* was something else. If Consuela woke up thirsty during the night and drank the rest of it, she might revert to age seven, and the mind of a seven-year-old in that luscious twenty-five-year-old body would never do. He cast an eye about the room for a suitable container. It came to rest on the wooden rack of chemical reagents above the work table. The bottle labeled Nitric Acid—Concentrated was nearly empty. He poured the last drops into the sink and washed the bottle thoroughly with detergent and tap water. As a final measure, to insure the purity of the fluid for future analysis, he rinsed the bottle and stopper with distilled water. Then he carefully poured the remaining *nepenthe juice* into the bottle, inserted the glass stopper, and replaced it on the shelf among the reagents. He rinsed the canteen and replaced it on the belt. Finished, he looked around, then smiled wearily. It was the last bottle in the world Consuela would choose to drink out of.

Scratching himself, Griggs climbed into the bunk next to Consuela's, tucked in the mosquito netting, and fell asleep, soon to dream of Nobel Prize awards, honorary knighthoods, best-selling chronicles, freedom of various great cities, television interviews and, when those pleasures palled, of the lovely and completely abandoned woman who lay beside him, snoring sonorously.

21

The room was like a sauna when Griggs awakened, awash with sweat. Sunlight streamed in through the cracks of the shutters, and the air was filled with the expectant hush of the African morning. He couldn't tell whether he had slept one day or three—judging by his weakness and hunger it might have been even more—but he felt fully refreshed, as he sometimes did when arising from sick bed after a fortnight wrestling with a tropical fever.

He swung his feet over the side of the cot and stood up. Weak, but fit. In the bunk next to his, Consuela still slept, heavily, like one in a coma. Well, he thought, let her sleep. By the time she wakes up, I'll have taken care of the housekeeping and we can think of more interesting things to do.

Grabbing his towel off a nail by the door, Griggs unlocked the door and stepped out onto the veranda. At the far end, projecting from the ceiling slats, was a shower nozzle fed by a roof-top barrel blanketed by just enough reed insulation to keep the water at a pleasantly warm temperature instead of steaming hot under the glare of the sun. He stepped under it, pulled the chain, and felt the warm liquid wash his cares away. After soaping himself thoroughly, he found that it had also washed away all but traces of the repulsive green fungus. Under it lay new, pinkish skin, like that of a baby. Another day, he surmised, and the infection would completely disappear.

Toweling himself vigorously, he went back into the house, hitched up a new butagas bottle, and put water on the back burner for coffee. From his wardrobe, hanging on a line of six nails on the wall over his cot, he chose his uniform of the day, a pair of ragged khaki shorts.

While waiting for the coffee water to boil, Griggs shaved off his beard and mulled over the events of the week during which it had been growing. The euphoria of the night, when in his dreams he had decorated himself, listened to his own applause, and kissed himself on both cheeks, dissipated in the sharp aroma of the percolating coffee. To be sure, the plaudits of the world of science awaited him, but there was serious work to be done and an enormous responsibility to be faced.

First of all, he would have to be careful what he revealed about the Formigans. It was a race to be preserved and studied, not displayed like a beast in a zoo, which would be its sure fate if he revealed the location of the grotto. In his mind's eye he could see Lindblad tours, T-shirt manufacturers, television-special promoters, zoological park operators, heads of one-horse college anthropology departments—like his own at the Black Athens of the South—and other fast-buck artists descending on the forest and its strange subterranean denizens. In a week the race of Formigans would be exterminated by their attentions. Only he could prevent that.

And then the specimens. The mycotic power to build vast bridges and crumble mountains by means of single-celled fungi, to mend ruptured cells (perhaps *human* cells, for all he knew), and to suspend memory—these too had to be investigated. But *carefully*, for to coax these rare and powerful genii from their tiny green bottles could be to unleash a demon upon the Earth against which the artifices of man might not prevail. With whom could he entrust *them*? Governments, institutions, individuals? No, for all these were susceptible to human greed and ambition, whom the powers of the fungi would corrupt absolutely. The answer was, he could entrust his secrets to *nobody*.

Once he began to think about it, he became a little frightened of the knowledge he possessed. With nothing more than *rodsume* and *emusdor*, for instance, he could revolutionize civil engineering. He could throw up great dams single-handed, build bridges across the Bosporus overnight, carve a new inter-ocean channel through Central America merely by scattering fungus as he strolled along. The curative fungi would put, perhaps, an end to disease. What then to feed the burgeoning world population, without a commensurately burgeoning food supply? As for *nepenthe juice*, it was the dream of dictators, who could rewrite history to their needs of the day: a drop of *nepenthe juice* in the morning coffee, and a *tabula rasa* on which to write the day's ration of propaganda. Griggs wondered if some of the same fears had afflicted Henry Ford when he was about to unleash the Model T on the world.

Yet to suppress these marvels was to deny his ethnographic discoveries credibility. Without the most painstaking confirmation by disinterested investigators, his findings would be dismissed as the ravings of a crank or one too long exposed to the boiling rays of the African sun. It was a dilemma and wanted consideration. The line between being hailed as savant or simpleton was going to be very fine indeed. But he'd have to toe it.

Sunk in his reflections, he didn't sense the near presence of Consuela until her shadow fell across the table. He looked up. She was still caked with mud, especially her hair and eyebrows, and she had thinned down considerably at the hips, which was no hardship, and around the bust, which was, but otherwise she looked her former astounding self. The Royal Red Fungus was gone. True, she was regarding him with suspicious eyes, but that was natural, considering that the last time she had seen him he was covered with that accursed green fungus.

"Good morning to you," said Griggs, rising. "Sleep well?"

"Like the dead."

"Congratulations on your resurrection." He handed her a towel and directed her to the shower facilities. "By the time you get back, I'll have breakfast on the table."

Breakfast consisted of canned peaches, soda crackers, a jar of sweet pickles, a can of cold luncheon meat, and a large pot of steaming coffee. She devoured it all.

"Did you tell me what brought you to this godforsaken spot, Briggs?" she asked, picking her teeth with a kitchen match after a breakfast eaten too single-mindedly to allow for conversation. "If you did, I forgot."

"Griggs. If I did, I forgot, too," said Griggs. Having feasted his hunger, he was now feasting his eyes on Consuela, who was sitting in a camp chair, shoulders against the wall, legs straight out and resting on another chair, nearly touching his own. Although she was as bare as a Bali maiden—with midriff not quite covered by the towel and breasts covered even more inadequately by thick tresses which hung to her waist—if she felt any embarrassment beneath the stranger's gaze she dissimulated it well. "I'm an anthropologist. I study the natives. And I sometimes suspect they study me, too."

"Very convenient."

"How so?"

"I mean, very convenient that here you are, and there I was, and somehow you found me right in the middle of the jungle."

"Oh—that. As a matter of fact, I was out on a field assignment at the time."

Assigned to shooting down Cuban helicopters, she thought grimly. But I notice you've shed your jungle disguise. Didn't mention that, did you? "I see," she said, and added with a tight smile, "I haven't thanked you for rescuing me."

"My pleasure."

"Speaking of which," she replied, fluttering long lashes, "how can I ever repay you?"

Griggs flushed. This was the other Consuela, the blustering, brazen bitch who had stepped out of the wreckage blazing away at him with a .45. He wished she'd go away, and leave behind the woman with whom he'd tiptoed among the stars that moonlit night on the veranda. "We'll think of something," he promised. "Meanwhile, I've got work to do."

"Going to commune with the natives?"

"Not exactly. I'm going to wash my hands of them. You see, today is the day I'm pulling out of this place. My tour of duty—my researches, that is—are finished. All I have to do is pack up, burn the files I don't want to leave behind, and take off. You're welcome to come along, of course."

Whether I want to or not, she thought bitterly. She could see herself paraded before the star-studded chiefs of the CIA, and this lackey being congratulated for having captured the paymaster of the Second Division, Cuban Expeditionary Forces in Africa, from whom they would then proceed to squeeze the secrets of the Cuban Army, with electrodes fastened to her nipples and other subtle American methods of interrogation. Well, she'd see about that. "Sure," she said brightly. "When do we leave?"

He went to the door and looked out at the sky. It was still morning. "In a couple of hours. We can make Ugeme before nightfall and stay there overnight on our way to Kinshasa. I know the chief."

"Sounds wonderful," she said quietly.

Griggs gathered up the breakfast things and threw them out the door. "Just got a few files to dispose of," he said, pulling up a camp stool to the four-drawer filing cabinets, "and we'll be on our way."

While Griggs took manila folders from the drawers, glancing at each briefly before dumping it on the floor, Consuela drank coffee and watched the collection of discarded paper grow. Most of it referred to diamond prospection, and for that reason Griggs was careful to place each paper face down; Consuela probably wouldn't know what any of the highly technical reports referred to, but there was no use taking chances.

From where she sat, at the table, she couldn't see anything except that Griggs was being very careful that she saw nothing. It was perfectly obvious to her that he was sorting secret documents which he would not risk leaving behind *or* traveling with, in case of loss or capture. Like a well-trained CIA operative, he'd burn them, stir the ashes, and flush the remains down the toilet. And speaking of toilets . . .

"Where can I—ah—wash my hands?" she asked.

"Over there," replied Griggs, pointing to the sink.

"I was speaking figuratively."

"Oh, sorry. Anywhere you like. No restrictions as to race, creed, color, or national origin. I myself give my patronage to the lee of that big eucalyptus tree back of the house. There are a few millipedes milling about, but I never saw any scorpions there."

"And?—"

"Yes—of course." Griggs reached up and tore a copy of the *American Anthropologist* away from the nail by which it was fixed to the wall by the door. "We've done a bit of comparison shopping," he said. "Pound for pound, the *American Anthropologist* is forty-three percent superior to the *Scientific American*. Not nearly so slick, you know."

When she returned, Griggs was stoking a bonfire in front of the house. The few papers he hadn't thrown on the pile were now stuffed in a brown leather briefcase lying on the hood of the Rover. These were obviously the most important of the lot, and she was thankful he had taken the trouble to dispose of the less sensitive documents. Saved her no end of time sorting out the wheat from the chaff after she had got rid of the mercenary spy.

Griggs prodded the fire until the flames had consumed the last paper—whatever he was, he said to himself self-righteously, he *wasn't* a litterbug—and went back up the ramp to the veranda where Consuela had been watching him from a camp chair. "Just about finished," he said.

"Wonderful."

They went inside. The fridge, stove, and furniture Griggs left as they were, on the assumption that sooner or later somebody addicted to such civilized appurtenances might happen along and be grateful to find them. The canned goods he had heaped in the middle of the floor. To these, the local gentry would help themselves once he removed the hyena pseudopenis from the door, where its magical powers had so efficiently kept thieving hands at bay.

So far, Consuela had seen no signs of weapons. Guns there must be, nevertheless, for no CIA man could do his dirty work without them. Perhaps the other two men Griggs had said were with him until a short time before had taken them. More likely they were in locked aluminum trunks next to the fridge, which Griggs had made no move to open in her presence. Wherever the weapons were, she'd have to contrive somehow to be alone to search for a gun, find it, and use it, for she had no intention of being trussed up like a suckling pig on a pole, to be brought a naked captive into the fleshpots of Kinshasa, for all the world to laugh at.

Griggs looked around the disordered room. "I think that's about everything. Except the hardware, that is," he added, jerking his thumb at the two aluminum boxes.

I was *right*, she thought. Now, if I can only get him out of the room for a minute. A minute is all I need.

Griggs winked at her. "But first, as they say, this message: can you spare a few pages of that *American Anthropologist*?"

"I left it out by the tree," she replied, scarcely believing her good fortune.

"Back in a jiffy," he said. He vaulted over the veranda railing and took off at a trot.

The moment he was gone, Consuela crossed swiftly to the aluminum boxes. They were secured with heavy-duty Yale locks. She was afraid that striking them with the hammer that lay nearby would bring Griggs on the run. Instead, she tried to pry the hasp loose with the antenna which she succeeded in snapping off from the short-wave radio. She was still working at the hasp when his footsteps on the gravel outside warned her, and she dashed across the room to shove the mutilated radio under some newspapers on the work table. As she did so, her eye fell on the rack of reagents in glass bottles, right before her. Cursing her stupidity, she grabbed the most caustic she could find, that labeled Nitric Acid—Concentrated, and thrust it in an empty coffee can on the sink washboard.

"What're you doing?" said Griggs, in the doorway.

"Oh," she replied, flushing, "I thought all this hot work must be making you hungry. I was fixing us a bite before we leave."

"Great," Griggs said. He pulled a suitcase from under his bed and started throwing his clothes at it.

From the mound of canned goods in the middle of the floor, Consuela selected a No. 2½ can of chili and beans. Opening it, she dumped the contents in a saucepan and put it on the fire to heat. After rummaging through the cupboard where the condiments were kept, she found what she hoped would be there: a large box of red chili pepper. She stirred the chili, some six or seven tablespoons, into the bubbling broth.

Griggs called over his shoulder: "How's it going?"

"Like a house afire. It's almost ready."

"So am I."

Thoughtfully she added the black pepper left in the shaker on the table, and poured her concoction into a soup bowl. She placed it on the table at which Griggs was already sitting, spoon at the ready.

"Smells terrific," Griggs said with anticipation.

"Just wait until you taste it." She stepped back to the sink as he dug in. He shoveled one heaping spoonful into his mouth, smiled, and then another. He was just plunging his spoon in the chili for the third time, when he let out a yell of anguish.

"*Water!*" He leaped up, wild-eyed, kicking the chair across the room, and jabbed a finger at his open mouth.

"What's the matter?" said Consuela calmly. "Don't like the flavor of my cooking? Too bland? Maybe I should add a little—"

"*Water*," he croaked, and dashed to the fridge. He flung open the door. Empty shelves mocked him. With a sob of pure agony he turned toward the pyramid of canned goods and beer in the middle of the room, only to remember the water tap. He swung around again, almost knocking over Consuela and the glass of clear liquid she held out to him.

He grabbed it, and swallowed it all in a single

draught. "Jesus *Christ!*" he panted. "What did you put in that soup, anyway?"

Consuela looked at him, frowning. This was not the reaction she expected. He was definitely in distress, but it was the kind of distress that comes of eating a few mouthfuls of chili pepper, followed by a glass of tepid water. She couldn't understand it. He should be writhing on the floor, tearing at a throat seared by Nitric Acid—Concentrated. The man's esophagus must be made of stainless steel.

Griggs' tortured gasps for air gradually subsided, and he stumbled to the sink where he put his head under the faucet and drank until the fire went out.

He straightened, breathing deeply. He belched. He turned.

Before him stood a woman. And what a woman: big she was, as big as Griggs himself, with a narrow waist caressed by lustrous black hair cascading over breasts as large and outstanding as the U.S. national debt. She was bare except for a rag of a towel around her smooth hips. She was looking at him strangely.

He looked at her lustfully. "Hey there, sweetheart," he grinned. "Where the hell did *you* come from?"

22

The wonder in his eyes was as authentic as his lust. Consuela had witnessed some of the world's great performances—Fidel, for instance, in full throat in the plaza at Habana, asserting with vociferous sincerity his independence of the Russians—but Griggs' obvious perplexity was clearly no act: woman's instinct no less

than a lifetime of coping with communist cant told her
so. So did his next question, a complete *non sequitur*
which demonstrated how complete was his temporal
displacement.

"Where's Gambino?"

"Who?"

"Dickerson—what happened to Joe?"

"I'm afraid I don't know what you're talking about."

"Come on—they were standing right over there,
packing their—hey!" His attention had been caught by
the pile of canned goods in the middle of the floor, the
neat pile of his possessions against the wall by the
door. "Would you mind telling me what's going on
here?" he said plaintively. "And who the hell are *you*?"

So he didn't know, really didn't know. And *she* certainly wasn't going to tell him. On the other hand, she
had to tell him something for, after all, he was still a
CIA mercenary, and sooner or later he would start digging into her story if it weren't plausible. She decided
to wrap him up in a bit of the same yarn he had spun
for her when she came riding into camp from the
darkness of the veld where he had picked her up.

"You've been sick," she said gently.

"Baloney—I feel great."

"I know you do—now. It's always that way after
you snap out of the fever. It's like you've never been
away. I know, because I've seen it before."

"You're out of your mind."

"No, but you were while you had the fever. And this
particular fever is often followed by a complete loss of
memory of what happened while you were sick."

"But I—"

"I know. You don't understand where I come in. Sit
down and I'll explain."

She forced him, still dazed, into the chair he had just
vacated. On the table before him the plate of chili still
steamed and sent up waves of fragrance. Reminded
him of something, but he couldn't quite get a grip on
it. But he was hungry, and he automatically picked up
his spoon and would have started wolfing it down had
not Consuela whisked it away.

"Hey!"

"See—you *don't* remember. When you made that chili, you put in too much pepper and burned your throat." She threw the plate and all out the door.

Griggs swallowed. She was right. His throat *was* sore.

"Anyway you're hungry. That's a good sign you're recovering from the fever."

"I tell you I don't remember any fever," Griggs said doggedly, shaking his head.

She sat down in the chair opposite him, her bare breasts looking him in the eye, so that he only half heard what she said. "You see, our group from the South Bronx Woman's Social Service Club was returning from a tour of the animal parks of Kenya when the plane apparently wandered into Angola—so the pilot said—and was attacked by Cuban MiG-23s."

"They don't have 23s," Griggs said. "He must have meant 21s."

"They do *too* have 23s," she flared at him.

He looked up sharply.

"Well, at least the *pilot* said they were MiG-23s. How would *I* know? Anyway, we lost altitude fast, and the plane crash-landed in the jungle out there somewhere—" she waved in the general direction of South Africa, "—and the next thing I knew I was alone in the darkness, strapped to a seat that had been thrown out of the airplane. My seat companion, poor soul, was dead—quite dead. Pity. She supported three children and a drunken husband. Anyway, in the darkness, I saw no sign of the plane. So I started walking."

"In the jungle? At night?"

"Of course. I had no choice. I heard animal noises, no doubt attracted by the smell of flesh. All I could think of was to get away from there before they killed me. I ran. Oh, I can tell you it was terrible."

"Sounds terrible, all right."

"I mean the thirst, the cries of the wild beasts, the thorns, the mosquito bites, the roots that tripped me up and almost broke my legs. Terrible. But at last I stumbled clear of the jungle, and saw this cabin in the distance. When I arrived here, the place was empty."

"Impossible. I've been here all the time."

"Empty," she said firmly. "You were lying unconscious on the ground out back, in delirium. I could hardly hold you down. As a matter of fact," she said, with sudden inspiration, for she didn't see why such a handsome and virile man should go to waste, now that he was no longer a menace, "I couldn't. . . ."

"You mean I—"

She cast her eyes down and nodded, shyly.

"Well, Jesus, I'm *sorry*."

She looked up, boldly. "Nothing to be sorry about. *I'm* not sorry."

His face broke into a fatuous grin.

She smiled. "You're a very insistent man, Maynard, and very strong. And fever gives a man the strength of ten. Thank God for *that*."

"I wish I could remember."

He really was quite handsome. And so long as he didn't suspect that she was a major in the Cuban Army, it didn't matter that he *was* a CIA mercenary. Once they got to Kinshasa, she was in the clear. There Griggs' associates couldn't touch her, for it was neutral territory. Griggs was something else: he could touch her, anywhere.

"When we get to Kinshasa, we'll try to reconstruct the scene," she promised.

"Kinshasa? Were we going to Kinshasa?"

"Of course, you don't remember. When you got up this morning, miraculously recovered, you said your work here was done and that we'd be leaving for Kinshasa the minute you collected your gear and burned the files you didn't want to leave behind."

"Is that what I was doing when I came to just now—burning files?"

She pointed to the mound of ashes outside the house.

"Then I guess I'd better see if there is anything else to burn," he said, his mind still in a fog. If he could only remember.

He went through the contents of the room, mumbling to himself, occasionally pausing to look at the girl. It seemed, after a brief inspection, that most everything he would want to take was already piled up near the door. True, some guns were unaccountably missing or misplaced. The Smith & Wesson .38, for some reason, was under his pillow. But where were the shotgun and the Universal M1 carbine? They had always been kept on racks, now empty, by the door, handy to deal with animals which ventured too close.

And the lockerbox with his notes. Doubtless that was already in the Range Rover. As it was his most valuable possession, he would obviously have put it in the vehicle first. But if so, then why had he found the last notebook, the one on Magenda ritual, on the shelf over his bed?

He scratched his head. If he could only remember what the hell had happened. One minute he was chatting with Dickerson and Gambino while they packed up their gear. The next, this woman had materialized out of nowhere, telling him he'd been suffering from a fever, for God's sake.

Those two locked aluminum footlockers by the drafting table were another mystery. They had always been used to carry geophysical instruments on field trips. That was Gambino's department, and Griggs couldn't understand why such valuable equipment had been left behind.

There was one way to find out. With a hammer he smashed the locks. He opened the lid of the first trunk. Inside was his shotgun. Of the carbine there was no sign. What had happened to *it*?

He shrugged, and opened the second footlocker.

In it were his missing notebooks, the fruit of three years labor among the Magenda d'Zondo, on which would be based the book which would make him a celebrity in the tight little world of anthropology. But what were his notebooks doing here? What happened to the teak locker in which he had always kept them? The mystery was compounded by a note scribbled on a piece of cardboard lying on top of the notebooks.

Neatly printed in bold characters, it read:

> When we saw the termites building that tunnel on
> the piling, we decided to help them along.
> Couldn't resist. Bet *that* scared you white, Griggs!
> Cheers!
> Joe and P.P.

It baffled him. Obviously it must be some kind of
practical joke. But shifting his notebooks from the teak
lockerbox to the aluminum trunk on the other side of
the room struck him as a pretty feeble effort. As for
the termite tunnel, that was a mystery. Not up to their
usual standard at all.

He carried the box to the veranda and put it in the
Rover. Whatever else he left behind, it wouldn't be his
precious notes. He took one last look around after having completed the loading and lashing down of his be-
longings. The room was a shambles, but there was
nothing left that mattered, except to the natives who
would come acalling the moment he was gone. He
pried the pseudopenis from the door, and tossed it
away.

Consuela had salvaged some clothing from Gambino's discards. They were shapeless, ragged and too
small. Griggs had to help her with the trousers and
buttoning the shirt, which took some time. . . .

Later Griggs cast one last look around the quarters
in which he had lived for three fruitful years. Those
years hadn't been very exciting, but he had solid, if
modest, accomplishments to show for them. His eyes
came to rest on the web belt with its canteen, sheath
knife, first aid kit, and other gear, and at the rumpled
and stained canvas bag beside it on the floor next to
the table.

"Yours?"

Consuela shook her head. "It was here when we—
I—got here," she said, although it *did* look like Cuban
Army issue. Probably captured from some other poor
devil lost in the jungle.

Griggs went through the bag. "Nothing here but test

tubes and plastic envelopes with some kind of gunk in them." They were undoubtedly biological specimens Dickerson had collected while prospecting and decided to leave behind. Griggs dropped them on the floor where he had found them.

He put his hand out to help the girl into the Rover. As she took it he said, "You know, I don't believe you've told me your name."

"Millán—Consuela Millán y Gorgas."

"Spanish?"

"Why, yes—how did you guess?"

"It's a lovely name," he said, looking into her dark eyes. "Lovely."

A moment later they were bouncing down the trail in the loaded Range Rover, swinging around the spur of jungle that stabbed like a jade dagger into the heart of the veld. But their eyes were for each other, and they scarcely noticed it.

23

Behind the eucalyptus tree to the rear of the house they left behind denizens of the rain forest were busy at work, providing a home and sustenance for their offspring. They were a congregation of *Kheper platynotus*, a diurnal dung beetle, one of some 2,000 species which clean the jungle floor of the droppings of birds, animals, and human beings. An industrious breed, the beetles—worshipped by the ancient Egyptians as a symbol of the solar deity, and immortalized as scarabs to accompany the dead into afterlife—attacked the small mounds of feces Consuela had deposited near the tree's roots.

Kicking aside the crumpled sheets of the *American Anthropologist*, each male beetle began to carve out and sculpt a marble-sized ball of fecal matter, which he would then laboriously roll away to a burial site. His forelegs straining against the ground, he pushed the ball with his hind legs, while his mate accompanied him in style, balancing herself atop the rolling sphere. Three or four meters beyond, the dung beetle stopped, and began to excavate soil from directly beneath the ball, which slowly sank out of sight below the surface. When the ball was buried the beetles copulated, and the female proceeded to lay a single fertilized egg in the fresh feces which entomologists have dubbed the "nuptial ball." On this ball the hatched larva would feed and grow into an adult, which would in turn scavenge the jungle floor for feces to maintain and increase his kind.

The process was swift, for competition is strong among the various species of daytime dung beetles. Within half an hour all the feces had been removed— to the last scrap, so to speak.

In its place now lay a handful of iridescent pebbles, blinking in the unaccustomed light after a billion years of blindness. The sun, sliding out from behind a cloud, smiled down upon them in welcome.

They winked back, knowingly.

ABOUT THE AUTHOR

For 30 years Daniel da Cruz has lived and worked—as a diplomat, teacher, businessman, and journalist—in Europe, Asia, and Africa.

He spent six World War II years as a U.S. Marine volunteer, serving ashore, afloat, and aloft in the three war theaters. A *magna cum laude* graduate of Georgetown University's School of Foreign Service, da Cruz has been variously a census enumerator, magazine editor and editorial consultant, judo master—he holds a second degree Black Belt of the Kodokan Judo Institute, Tokyo—taxi driver, public relations officer for an oil company, salesman, foreign correspondent, publishers' representative, vice-president of a New York advertising agency, slaughterhouse skinner, American Embassy press attaché in Baghdad, and copper miner. He is currently Adjunct Professor of Anthropology at Miami University.

da Cruz has published ten books, among them an American history text, a monograph on Amerindian linguistics, and three suspense novels for Ballantine Books, the most recent of which, *The Captive City*, was awarded a special "Edgar."